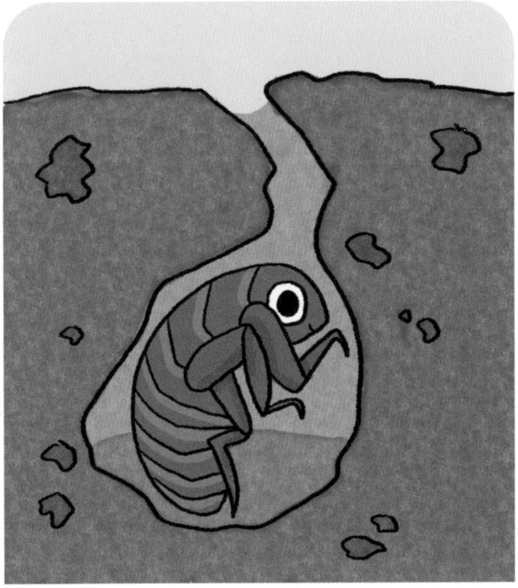

ROOM TO GROW

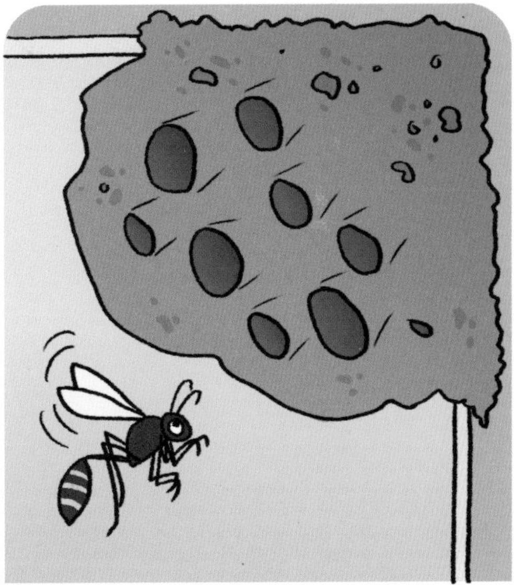

CORNER LOT

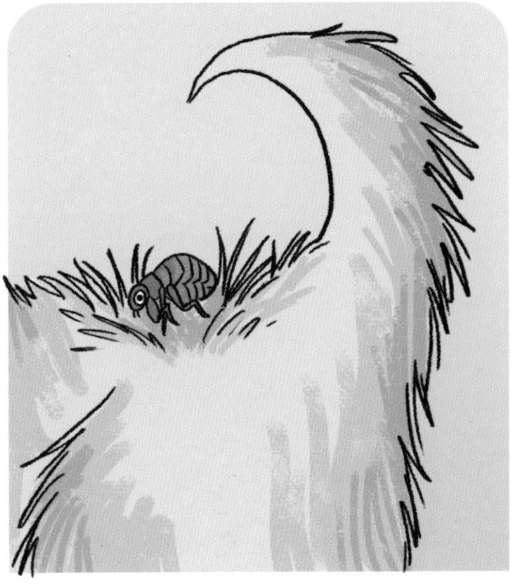

OPEN FLOOR PLAN

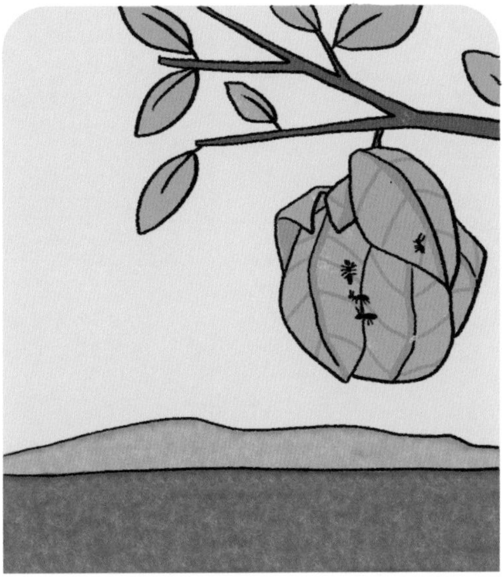

STUNNING VIEWS

Ashley Spires

BURT THE BEETLE LIVES HERE!

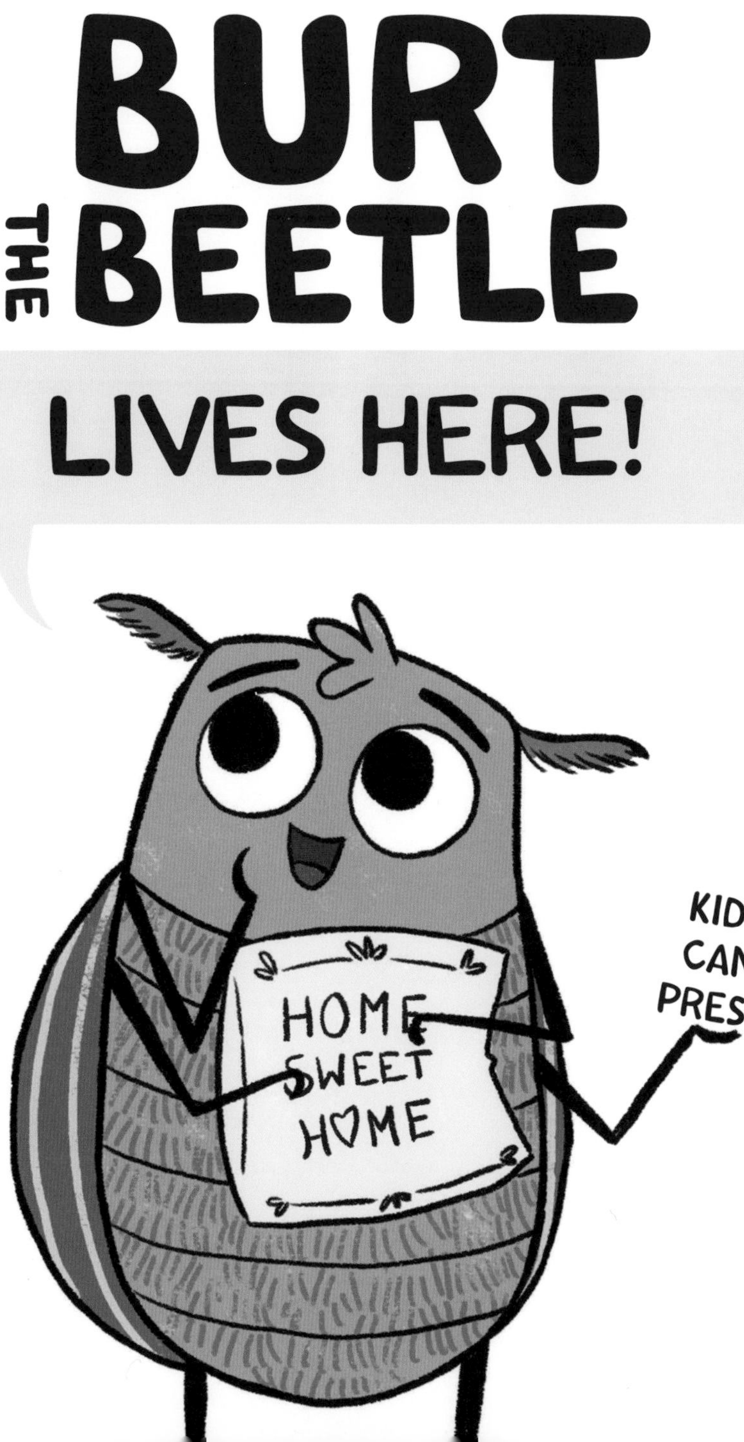
HOME
SWEET
HOME

KIDS CAN PRESS

INSECTS LIVE IN EVERY CORNER OF THE PLANET.

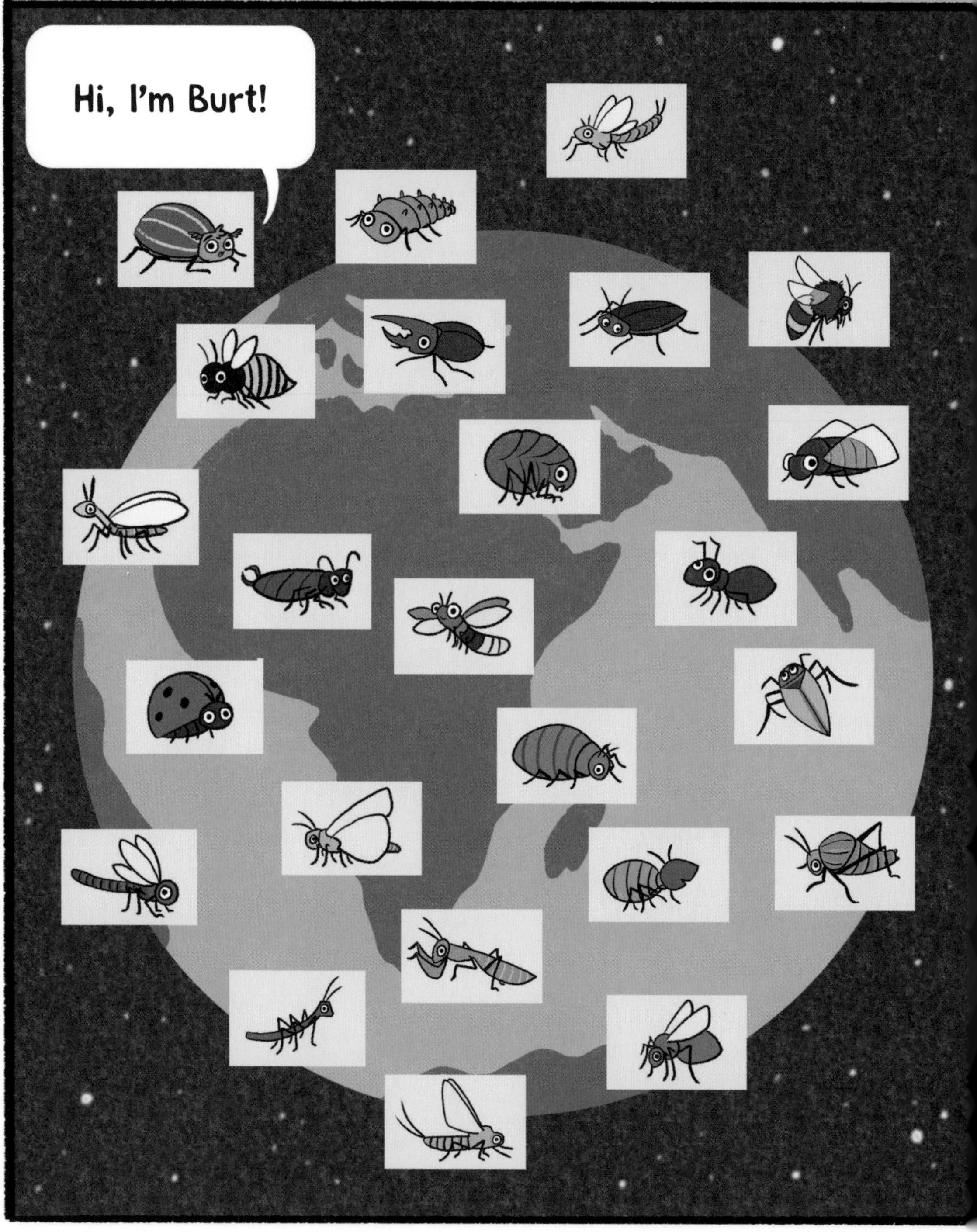
Hi, I'm Burt!

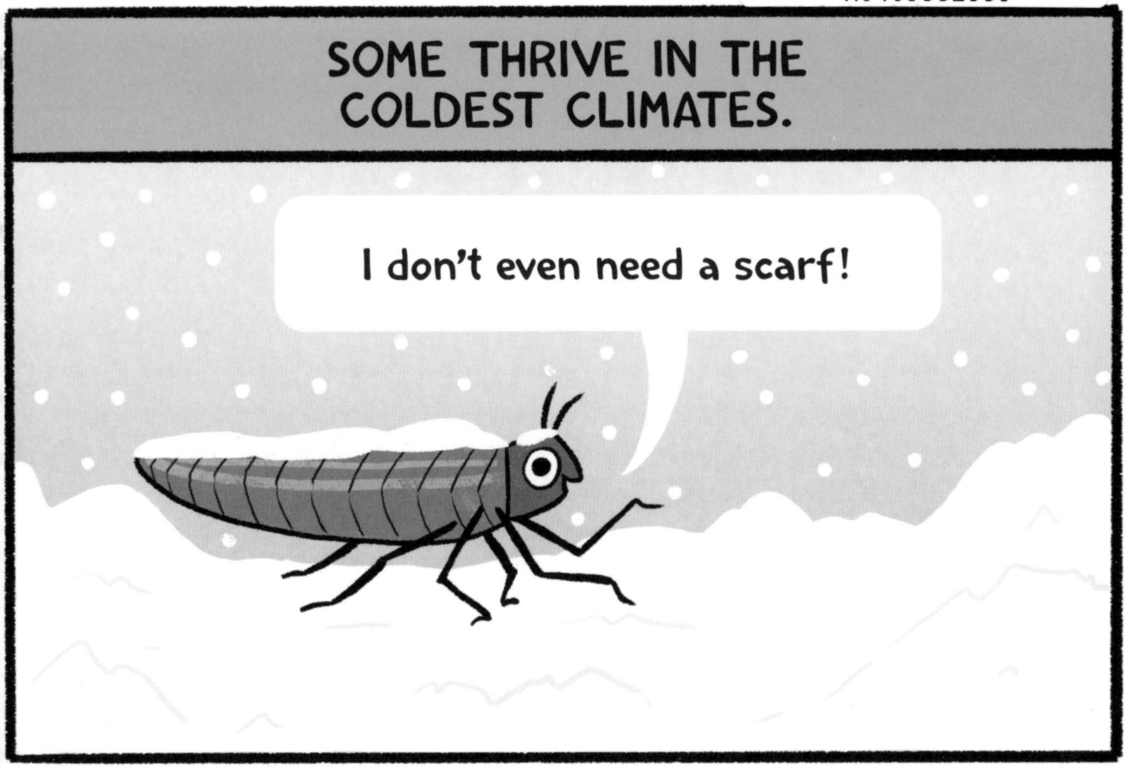
SOME THRIVE IN THE COLDEST CLIMATES.
I don't even need a scarf!

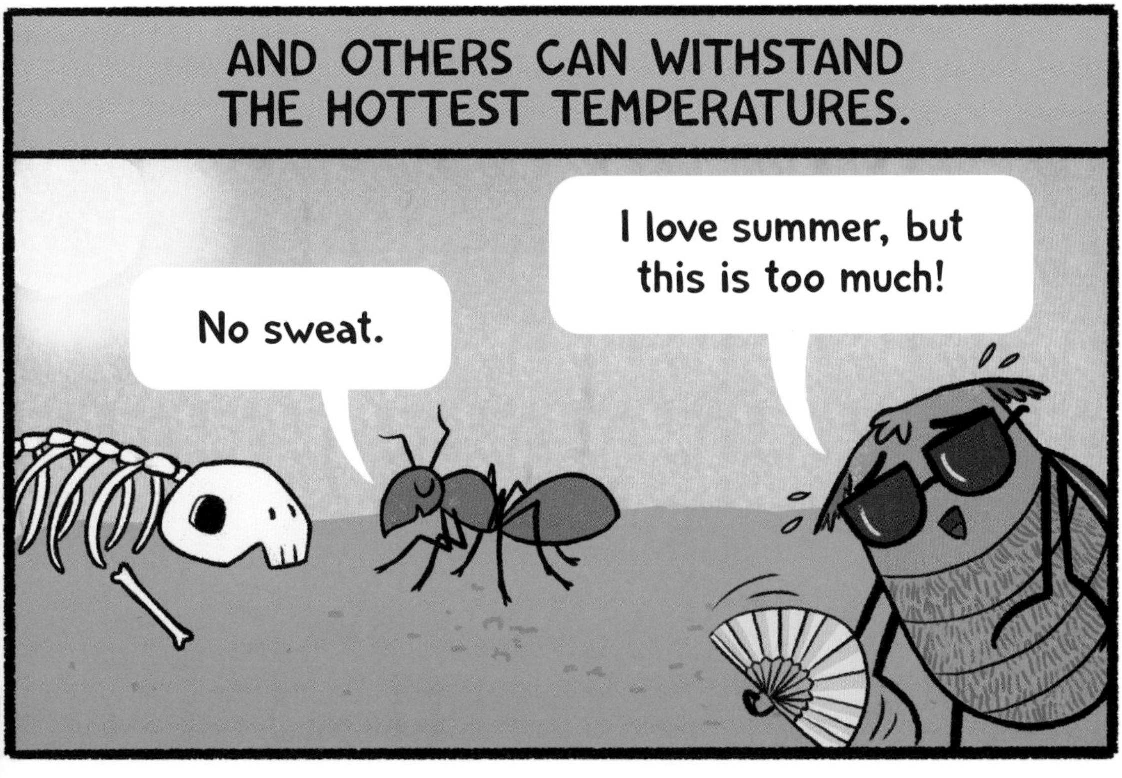
AND OTHERS CAN WITHSTAND THE HOTTEST TEMPERATURES.
No sweat.
I love summer, but this is too much!

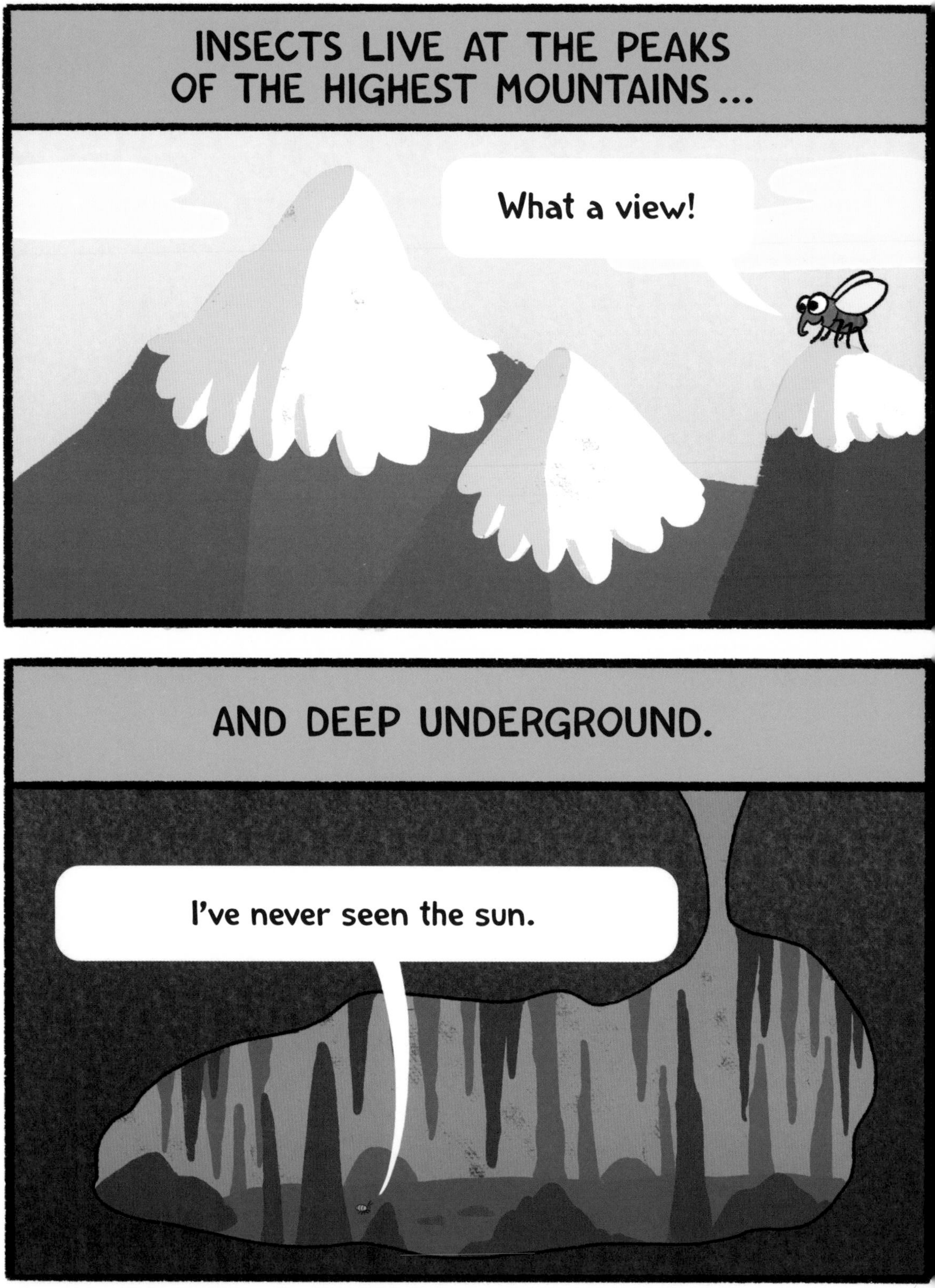
INSECTS LIVE AT THE PEAKS OF THE HIGHEST MOUNTAINS...
What a view!
AND DEEP UNDERGROUND.
I've never seen the sun.

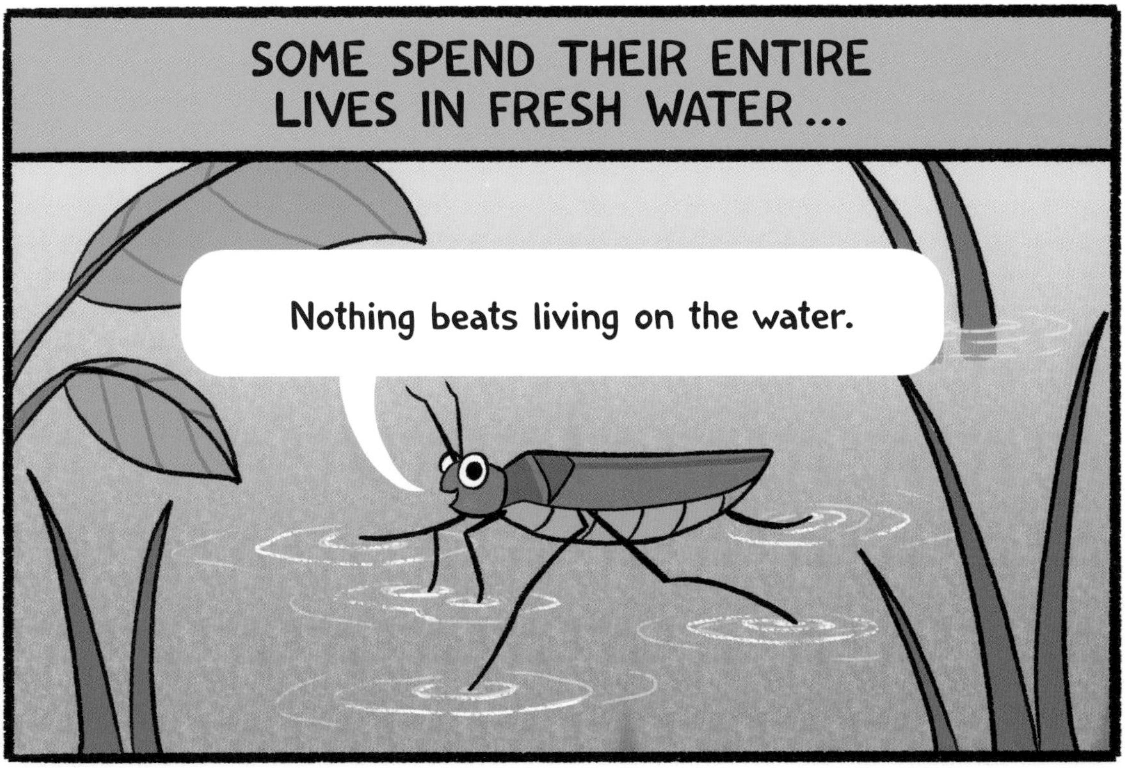
SOME SPEND THEIR ENTIRE LIVES IN FRESH WATER...
Nothing beats living on the water.

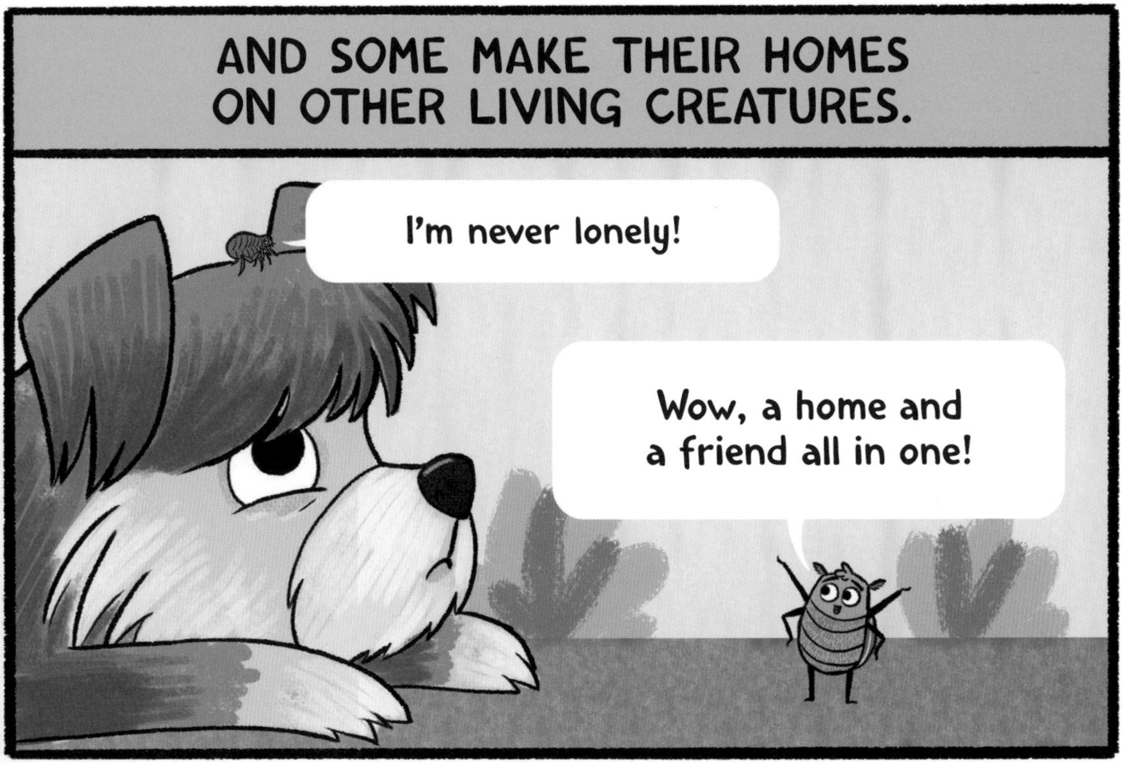
AND SOME MAKE THEIR HOMES ON OTHER LIVING CREATURES.
I'm never lonely!
Wow, a home and a friend all in one!

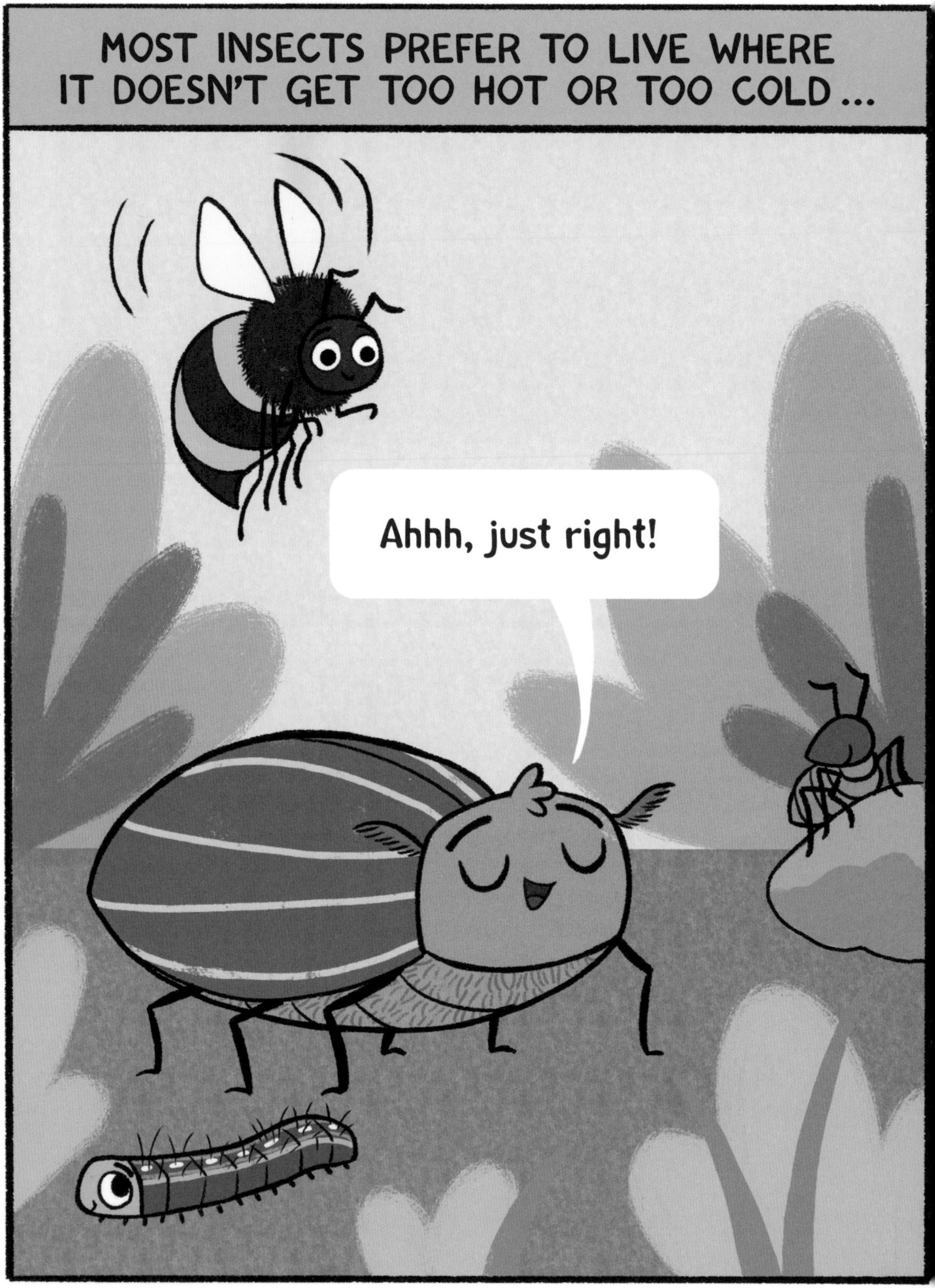
MOST INSECTS PREFER TO LIVE WHERE IT DOESN'T GET TOO HOT OR TOO COLD...
Ahhh, just right!

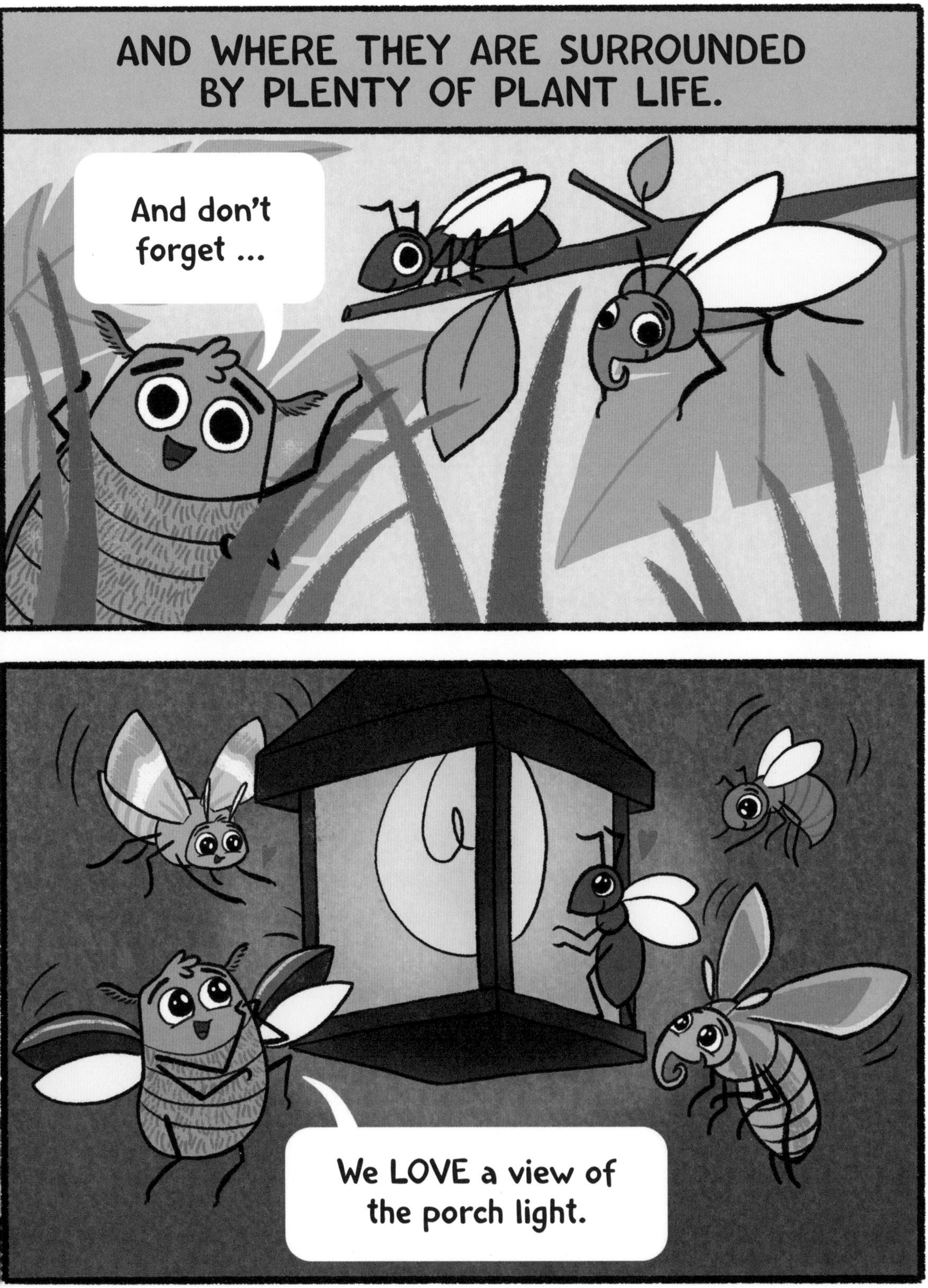
AND WHERE THEY ARE SURROUNDED BY PLENTY OF PLANT LIFE.
And don't forget ...
We LOVE a view of the porch light.

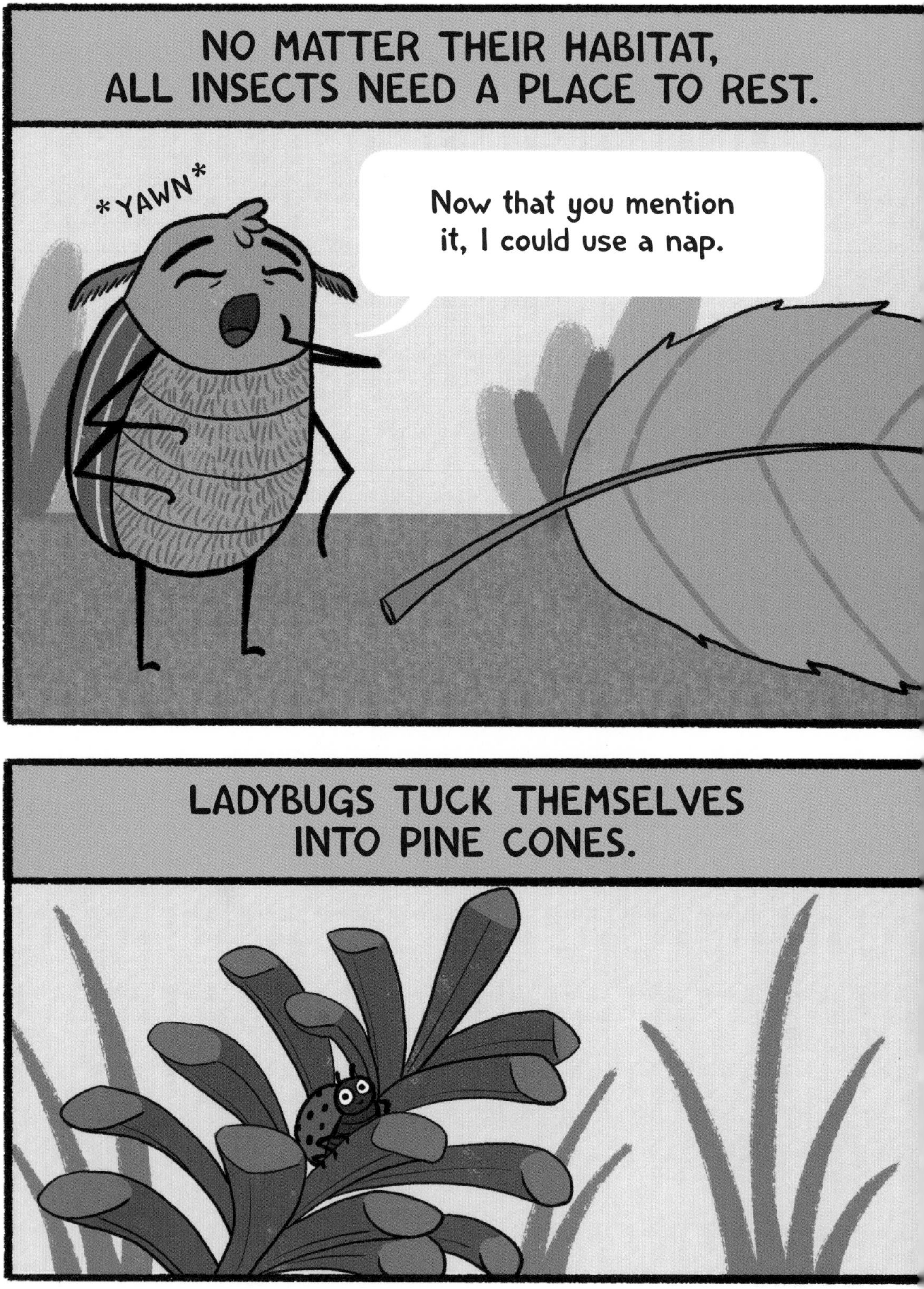
NO MATTER THEIR HABITAT, ALL INSECTS NEED A PLACE TO REST.
YAWN
Now that you mention it, I could use a nap.
LADYBUGS TUCK THEMSELVES INTO PINE CONES.

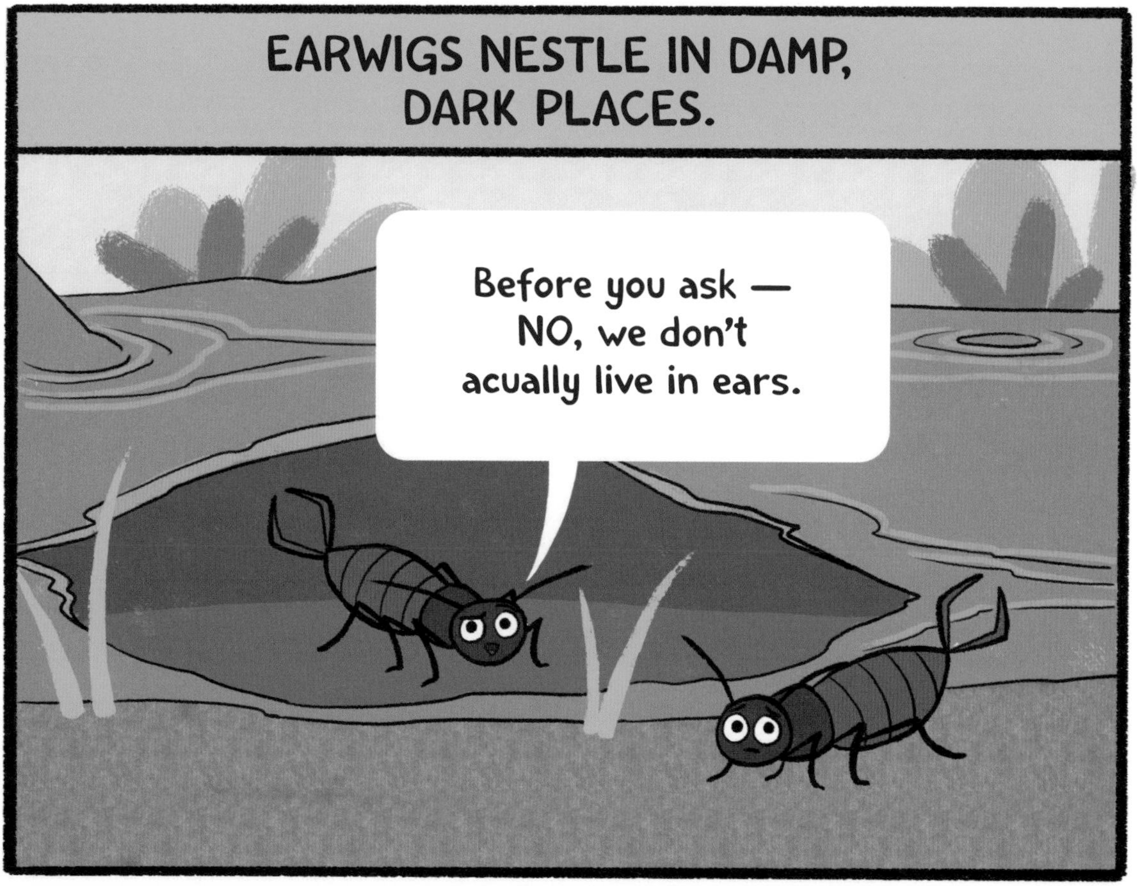
EARWIGS NESTLE IN DAMP, DARK PLACES.
Before you ask — NO, we don't acually live in ears.

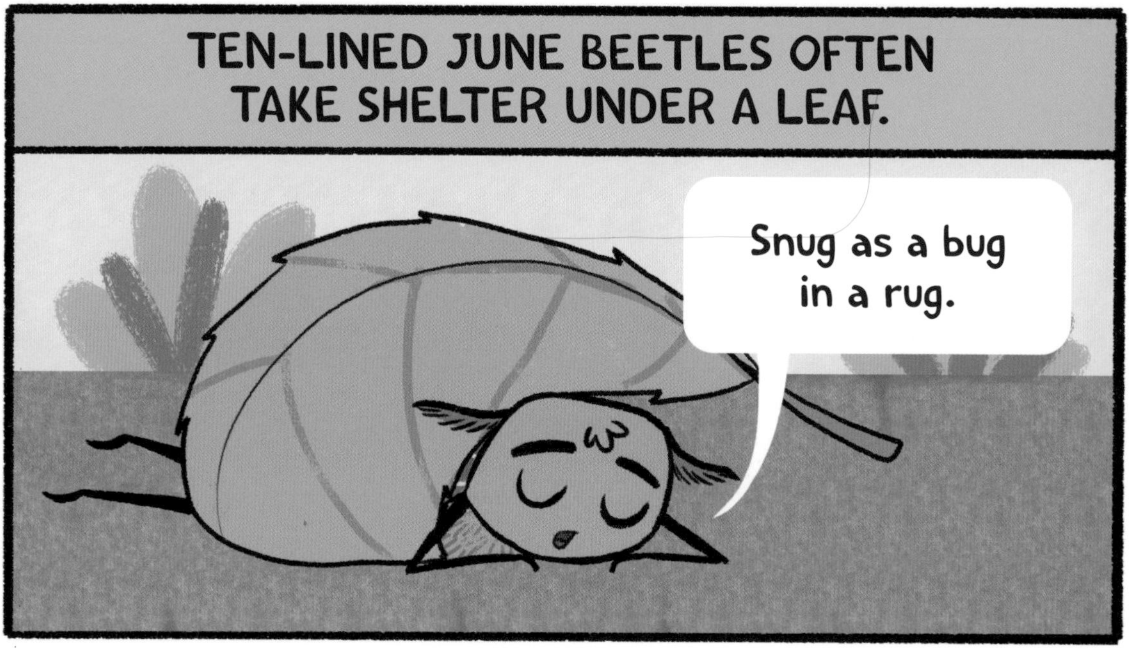
TEN-LINED JUNE BEETLES OFTEN TAKE SHELTER UNDER A LEAF.
Snug as a bug in a rug.

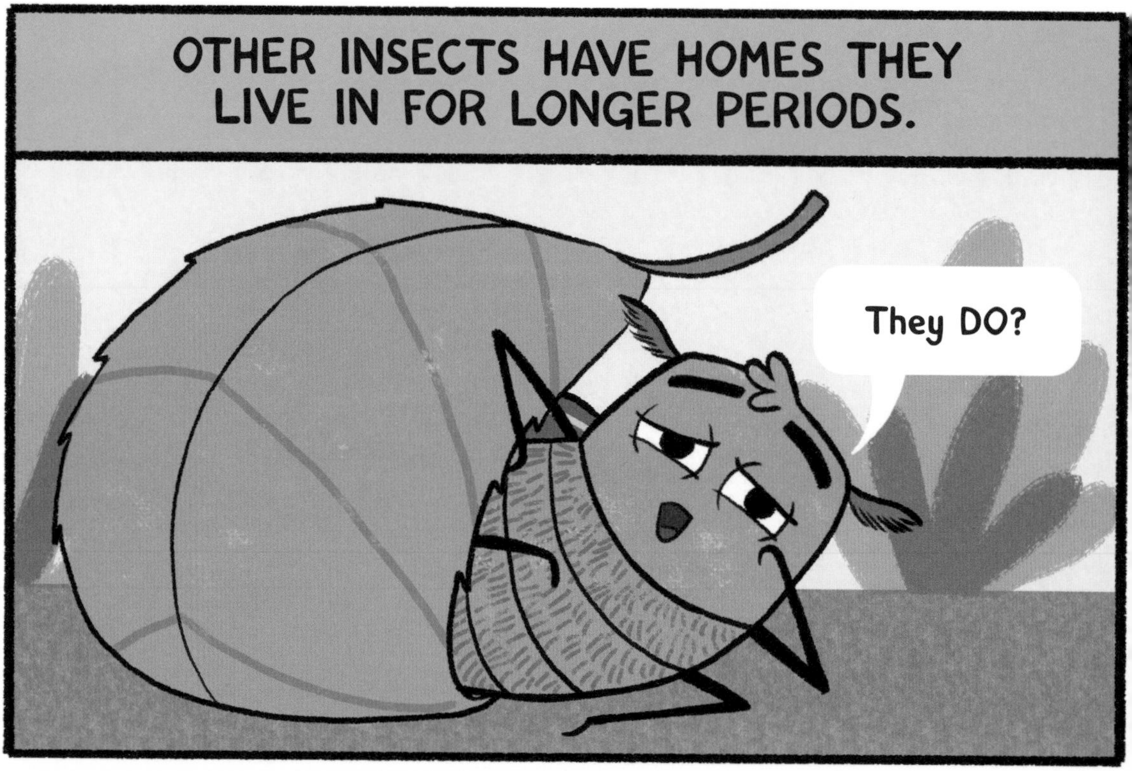
OTHER INSECTS HAVE HOMES THEY LIVE IN FOR LONGER PERIODS.
They DO?

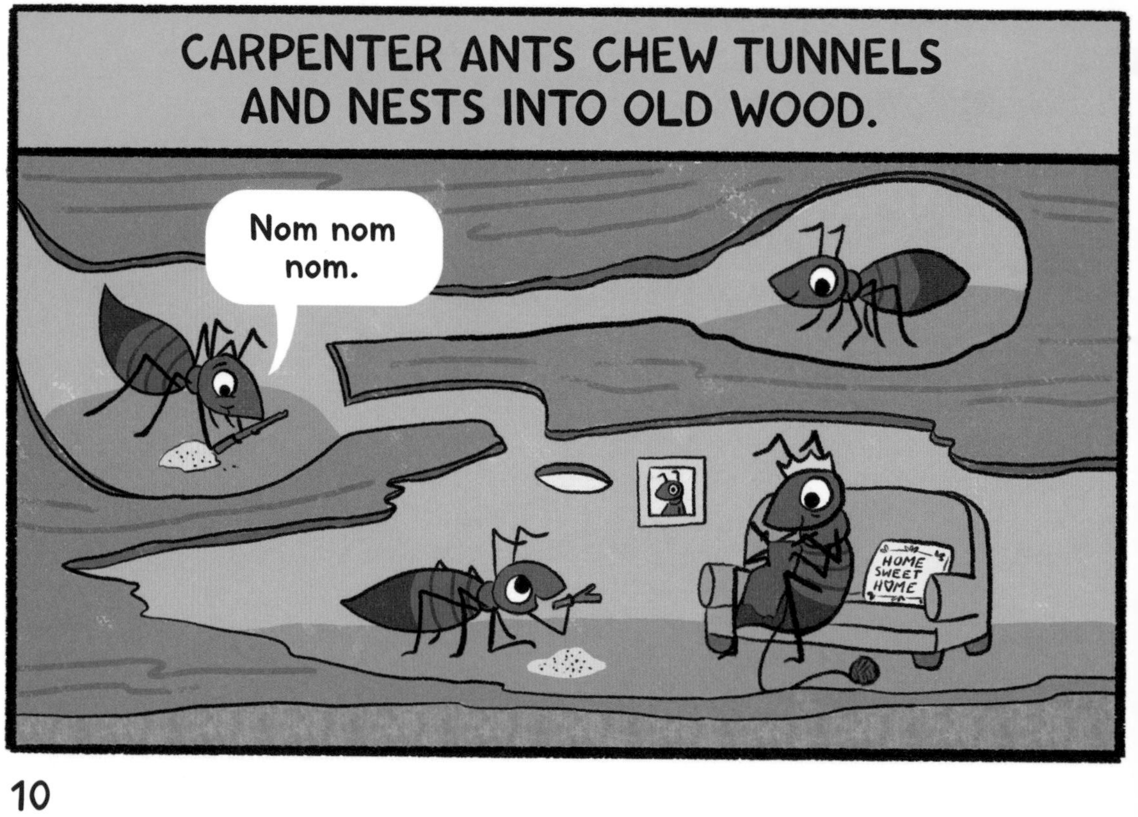
CARPENTER ANTS CHEW TUNNELS AND NESTS INTO OLD WOOD.
Nom nom nom.
HOME SWEET HOME

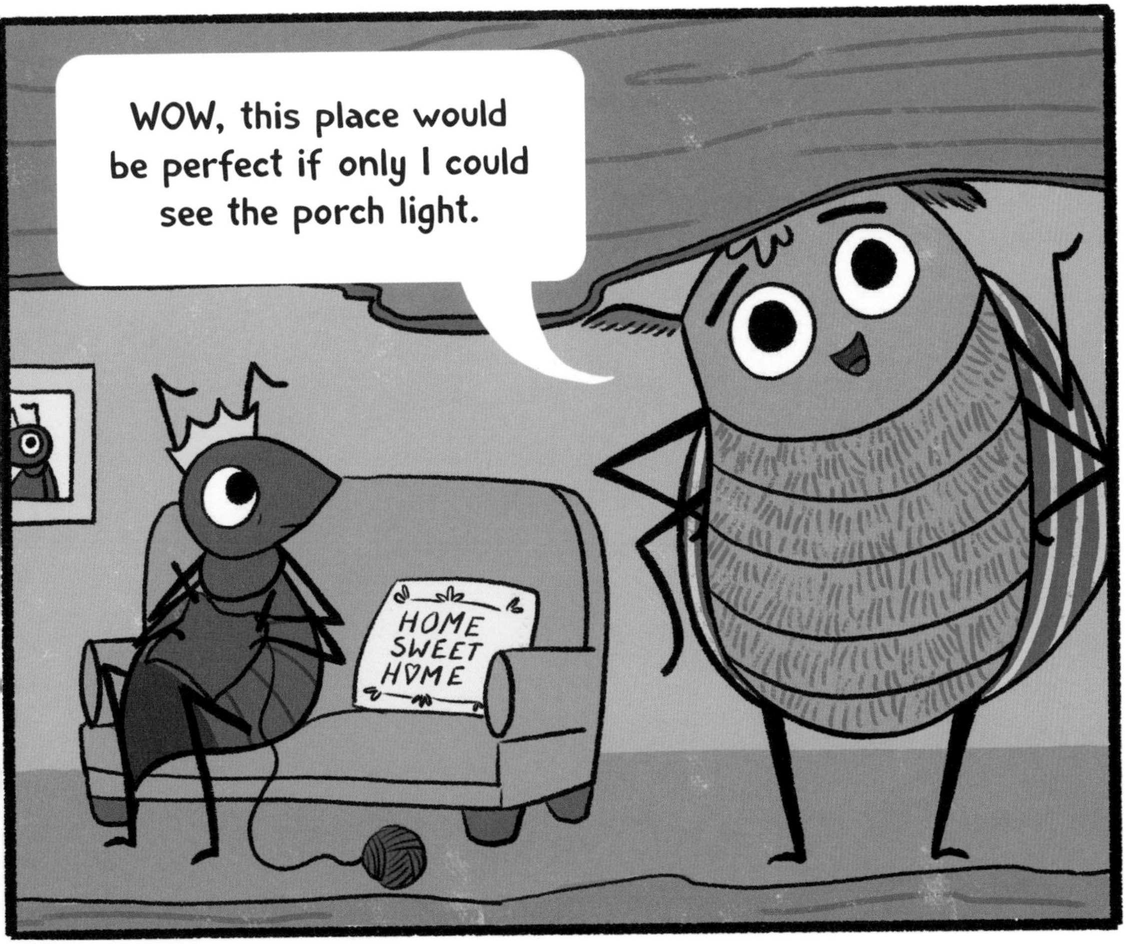
WOW, this place would be perfect if only I could see the porch light.
HOME SWEET HOME

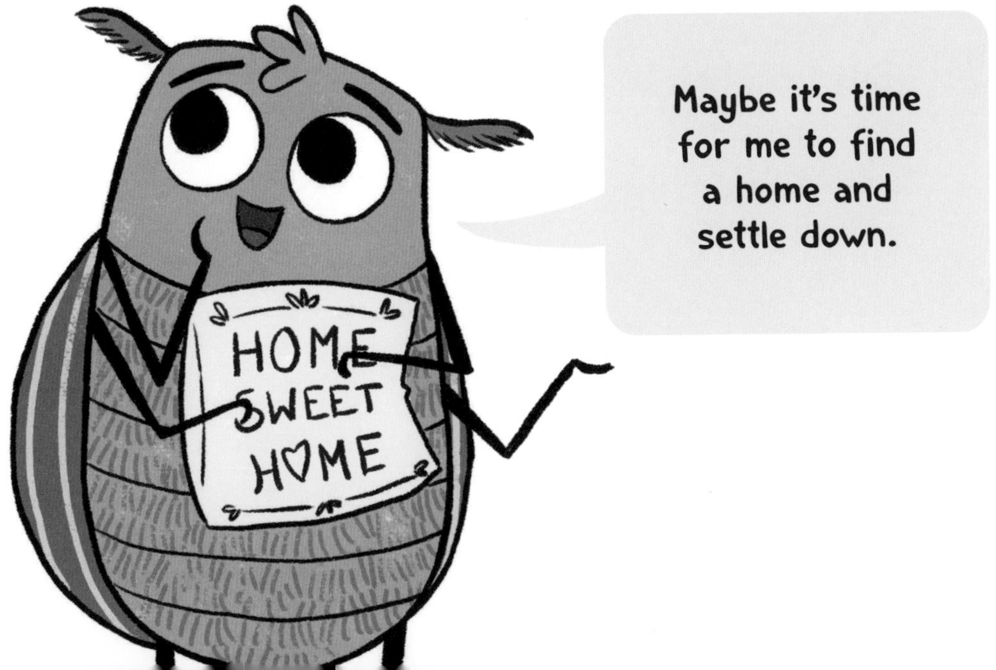
Maybe it's time for me to find a home and settle down.
HOME SWEET HOME

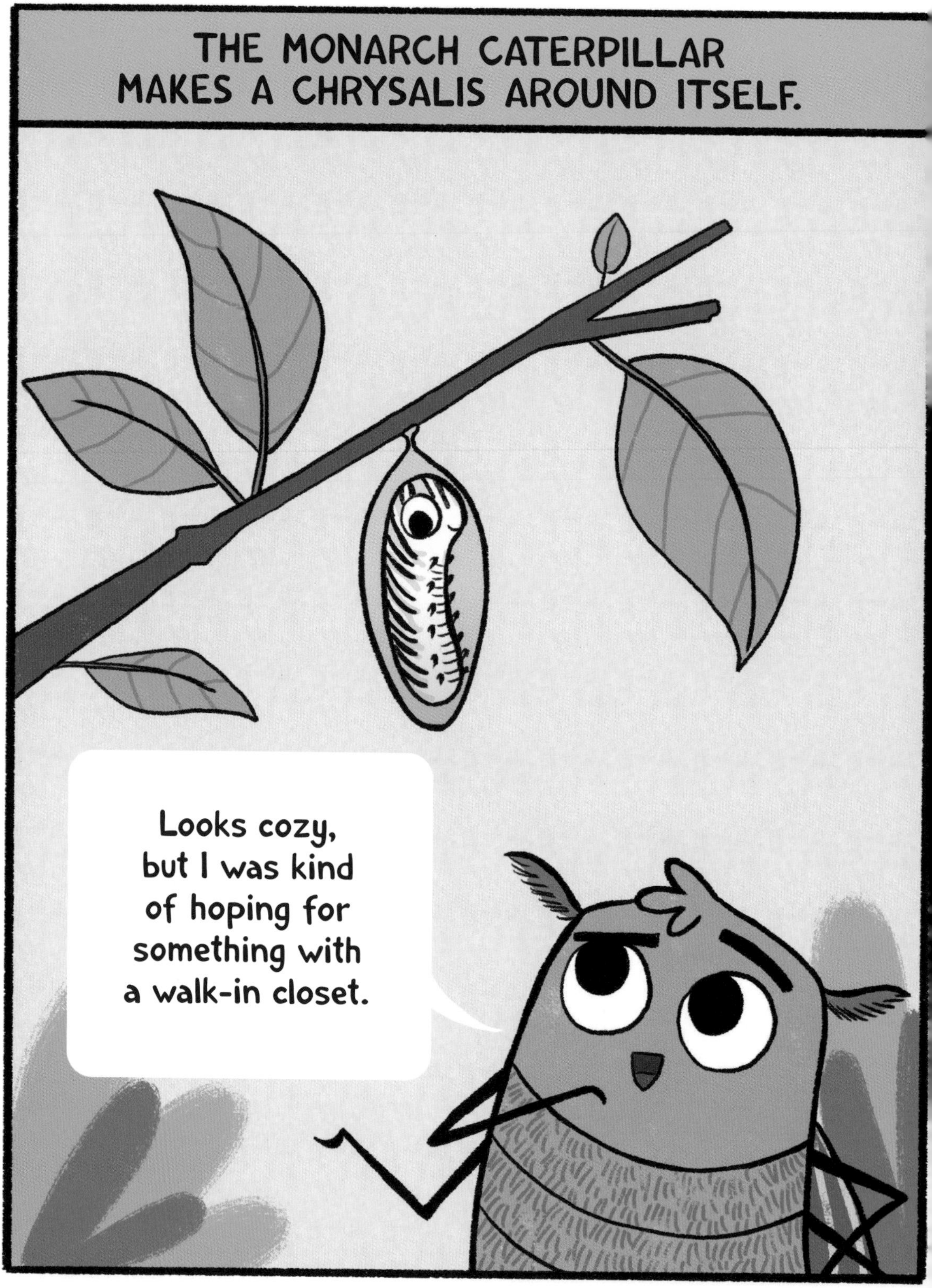
THE MONARCH CATERPILLAR MAKES A CHRYSALIS AROUND ITSELF.
Looks cozy, but I was kind of hoping for something with a walk-in closet.

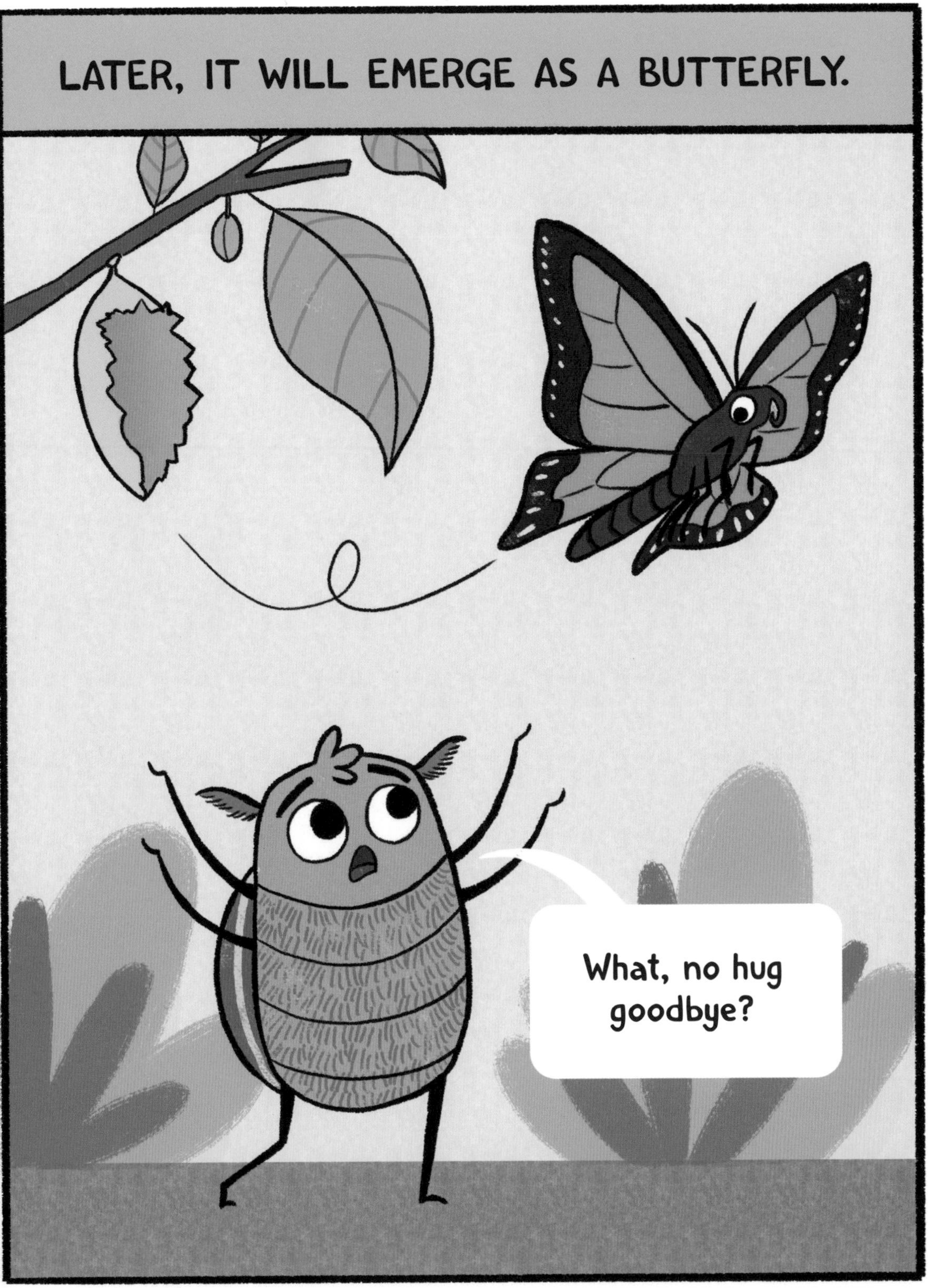
LATER, IT WILL EMERGE AS A BUTTERFLY.
What, no hug goodbye?

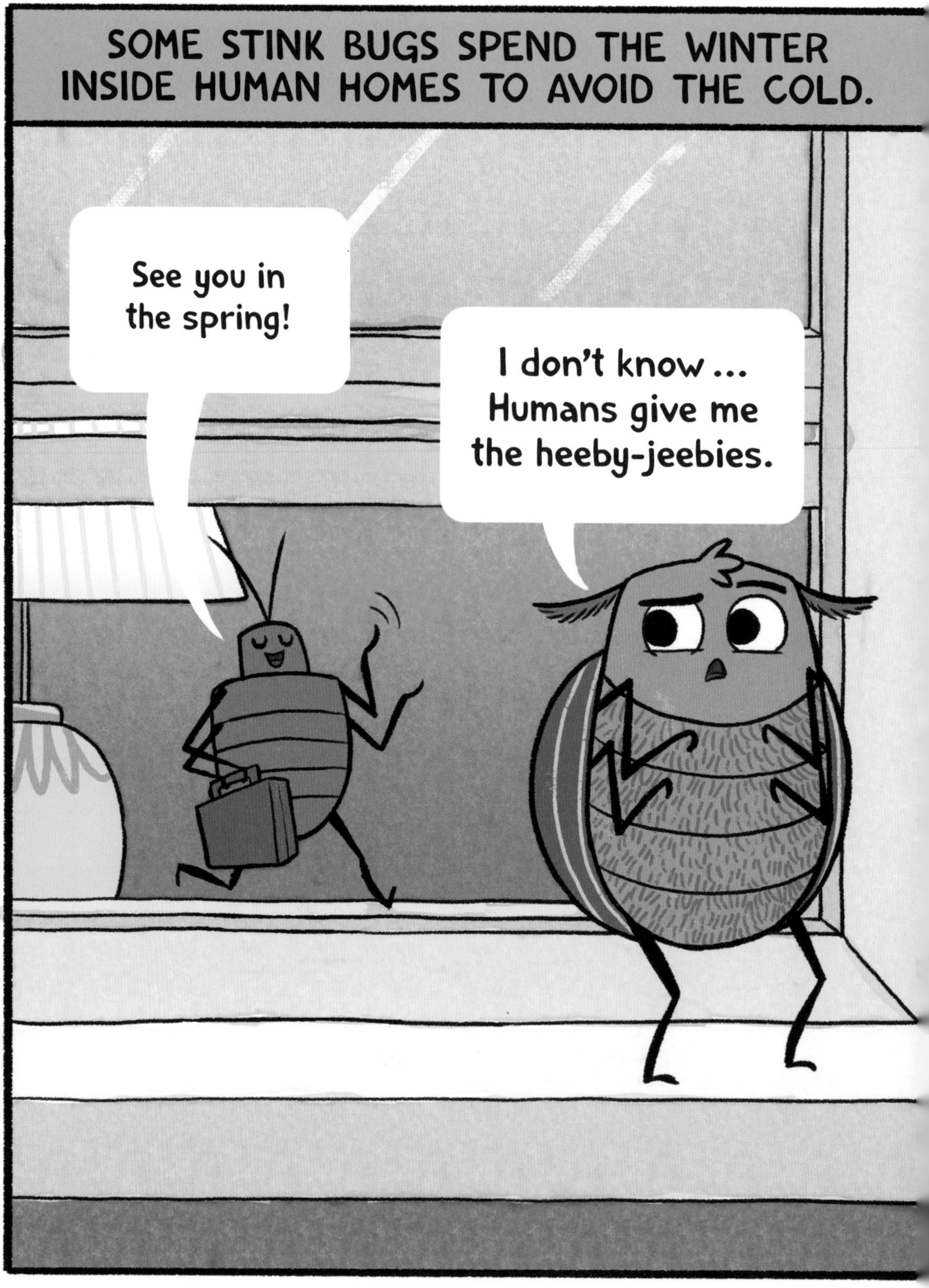
SOME STINK BUGS SPEND THE WINTER INSIDE HUMAN HOMES TO AVOID THE COLD.
See you in the spring!
I don't know ... Humans give me the heeby-jeebies.

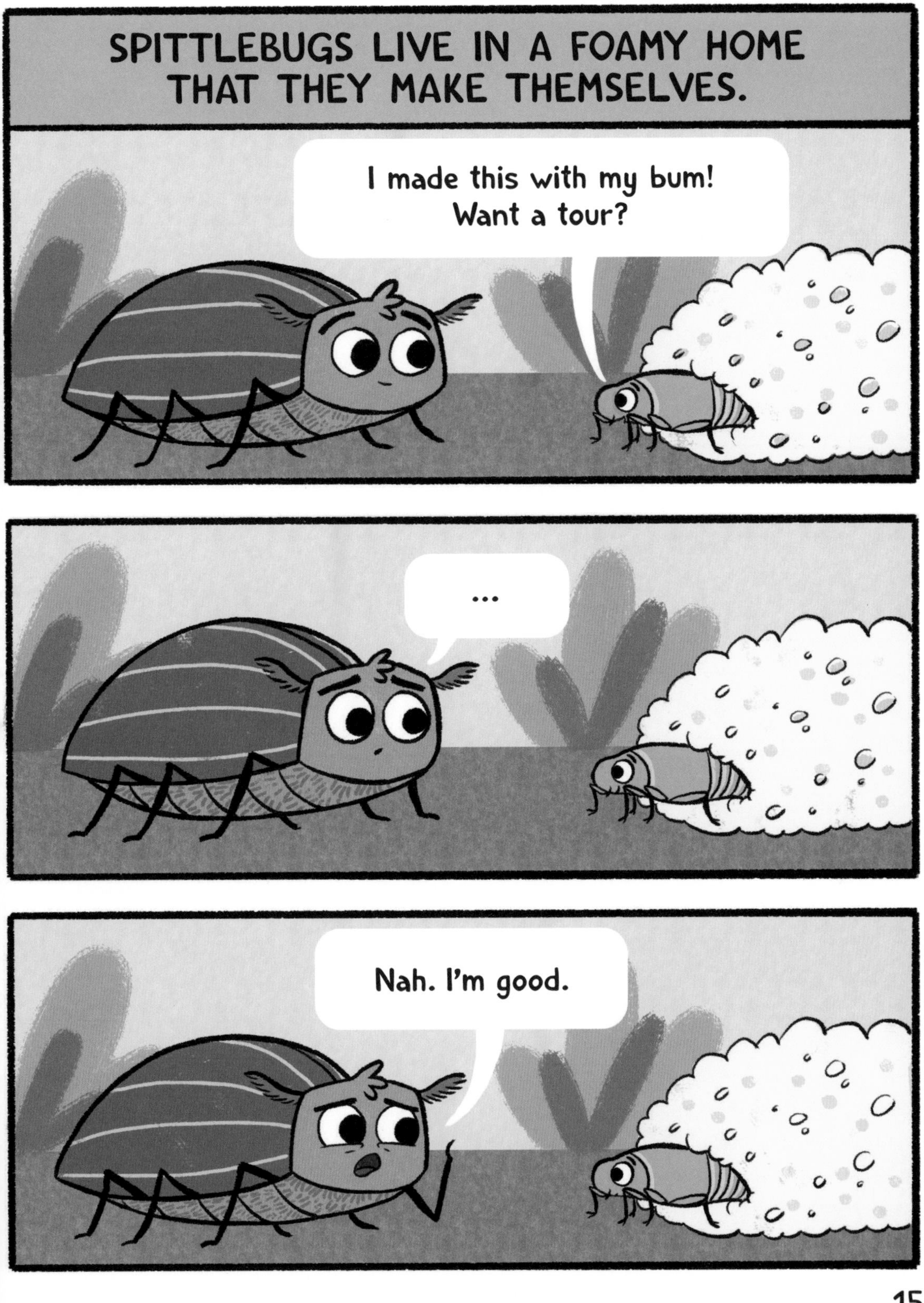
SPITTLEBUGS LIVE IN A FOAMY HOME THAT THEY MAKE THEMSELVES.
I made this with my bum! Want a tour?
...
Nah. I'm good.

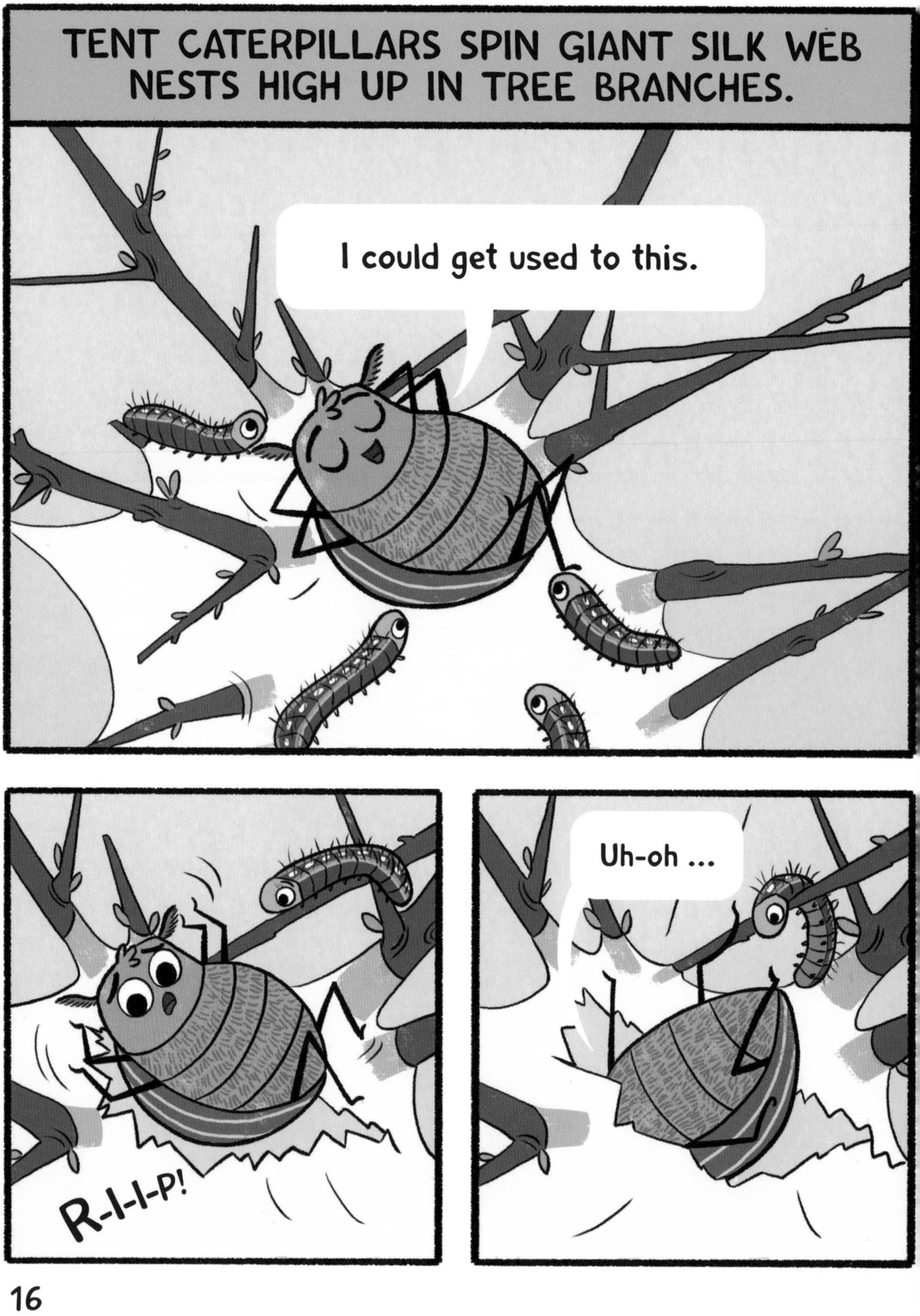
TENT CATERPILLARS SPIN GIANT SILK WEB NESTS HIGH UP IN TREE BRANCHES.
I could get used to this.
R-I-I-P!
Uh-oh ...

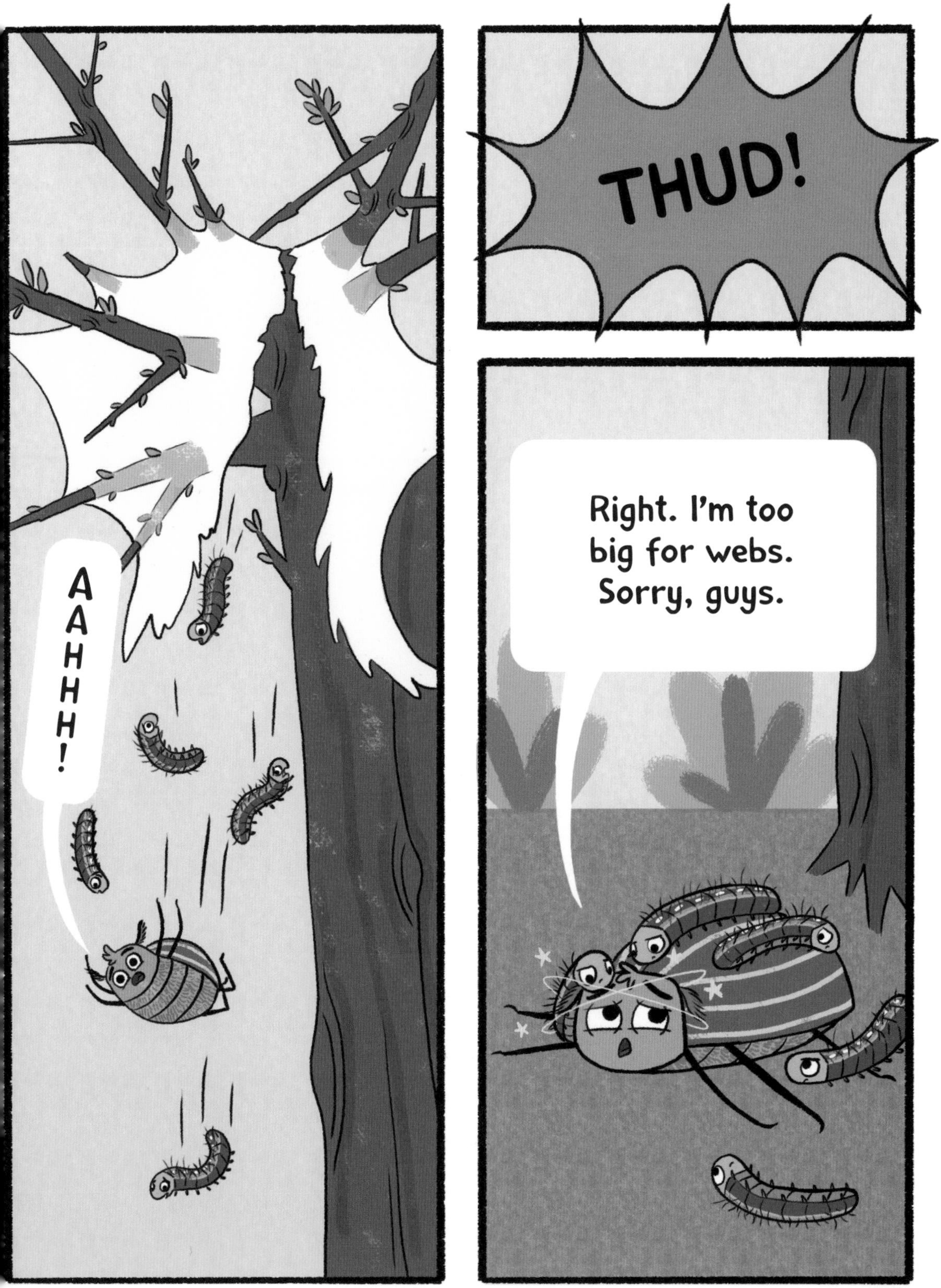
AAHHHH!
THUD!
Right. I'm too big for webs. Sorry, guys.

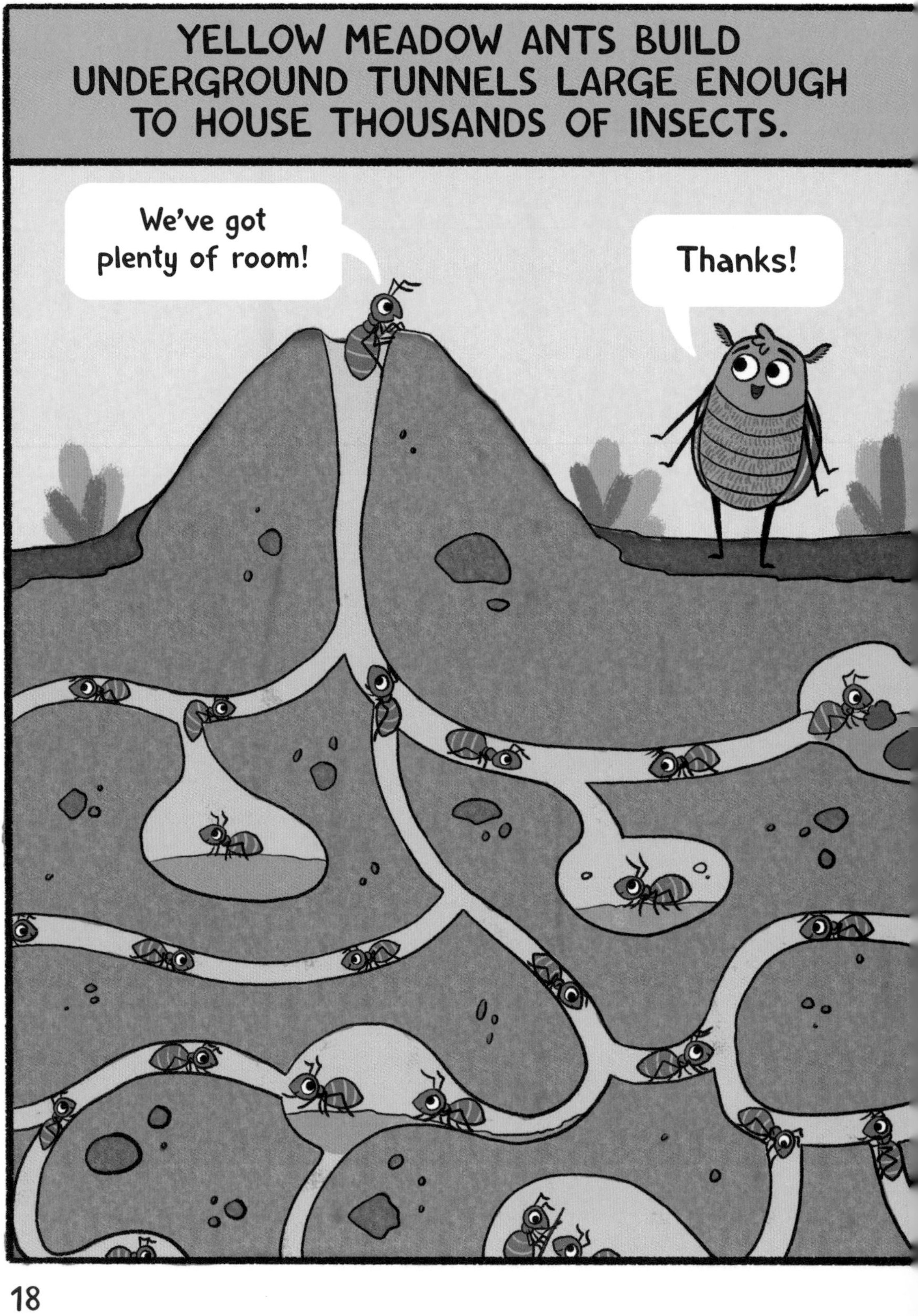
YELLOW MEADOW ANTS BUILD UNDERGROUND TUNNELS LARGE ENOUGH TO HOUSE THOUSANDS OF INSECTS.
We've got plenty of room!
Thanks!

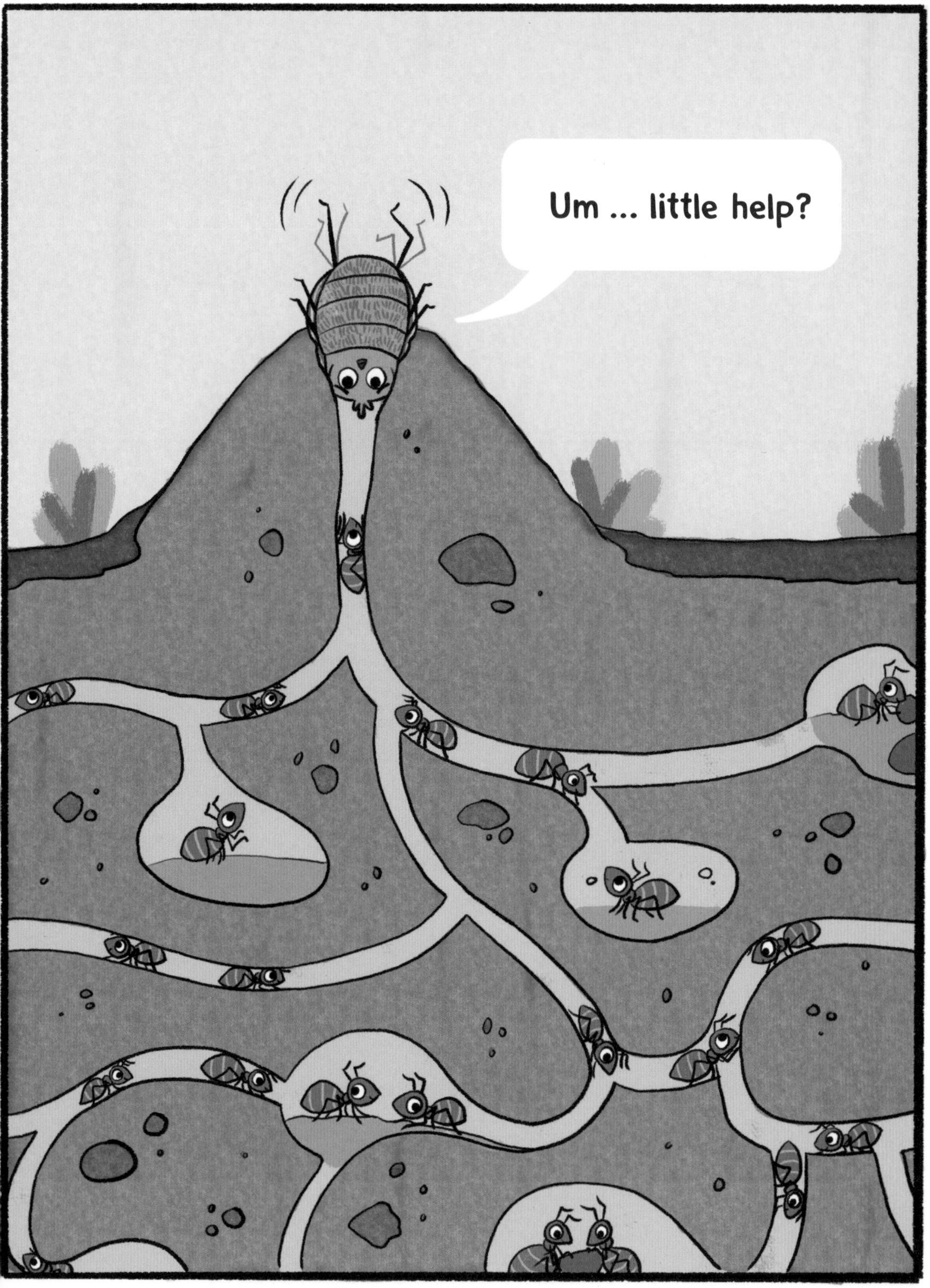
Um ... little help?

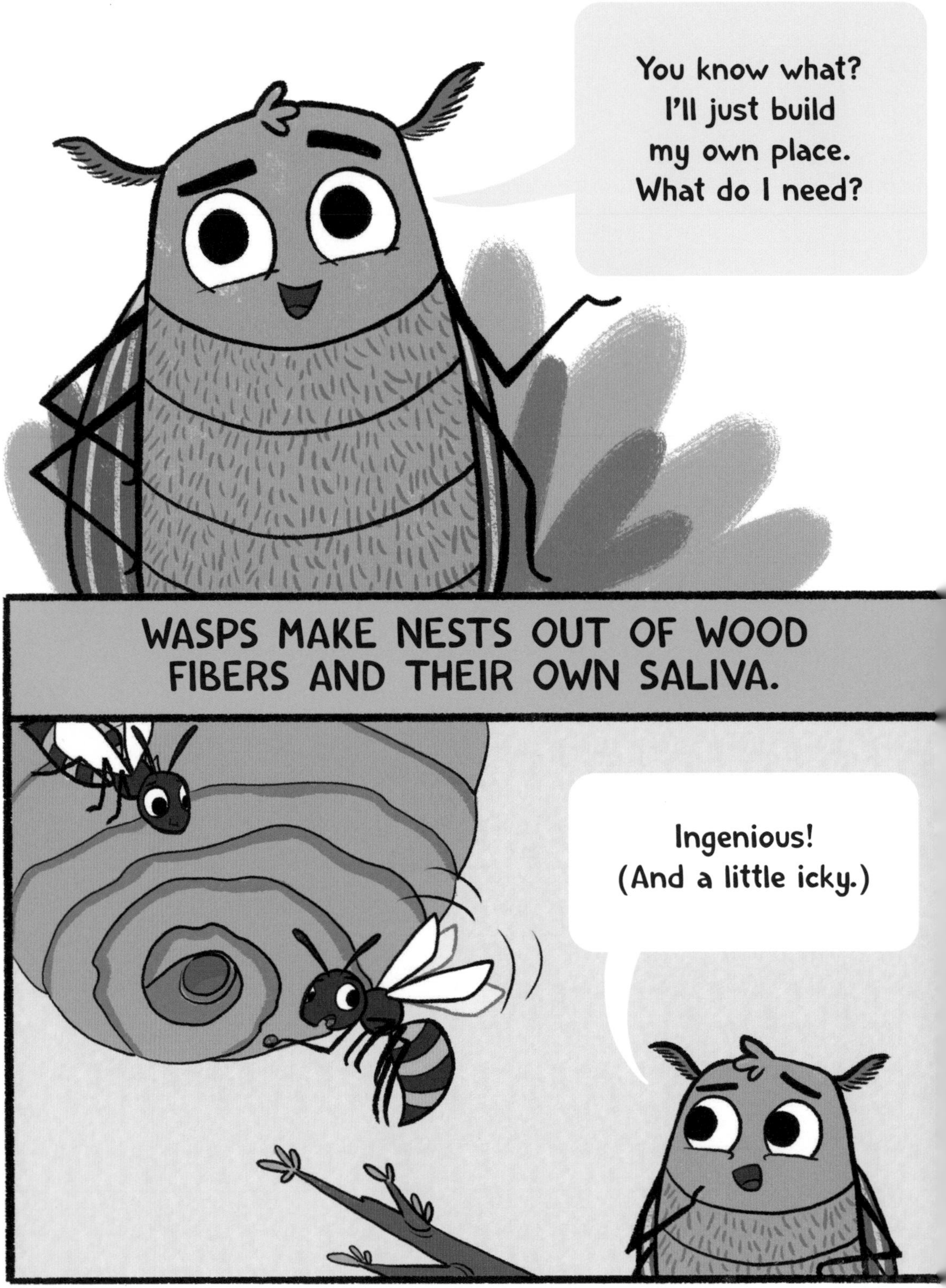
You know what? I'll just build my own place. What do I need?
WASPS MAKE NESTS OUT OF WOOD FIBERS AND THEIR OWN SALIVA.
Ingenious! (And a little icky.)

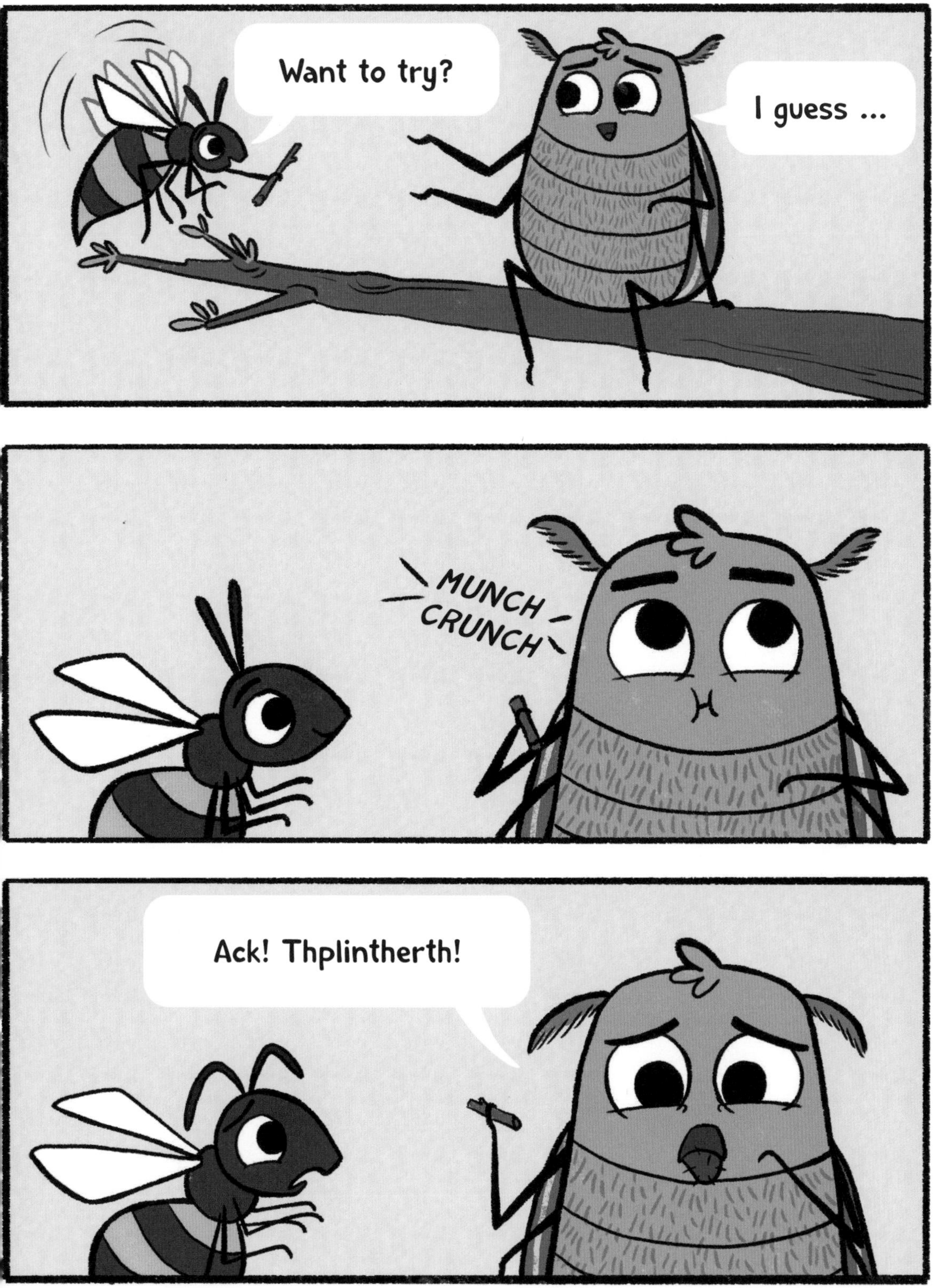
Want to try?
I guess ...
MUNCH
CRUNCH
Ack! Thplintherth!

BEES BUILD MATHEMATICALLY PERFECT WAX HIVES.

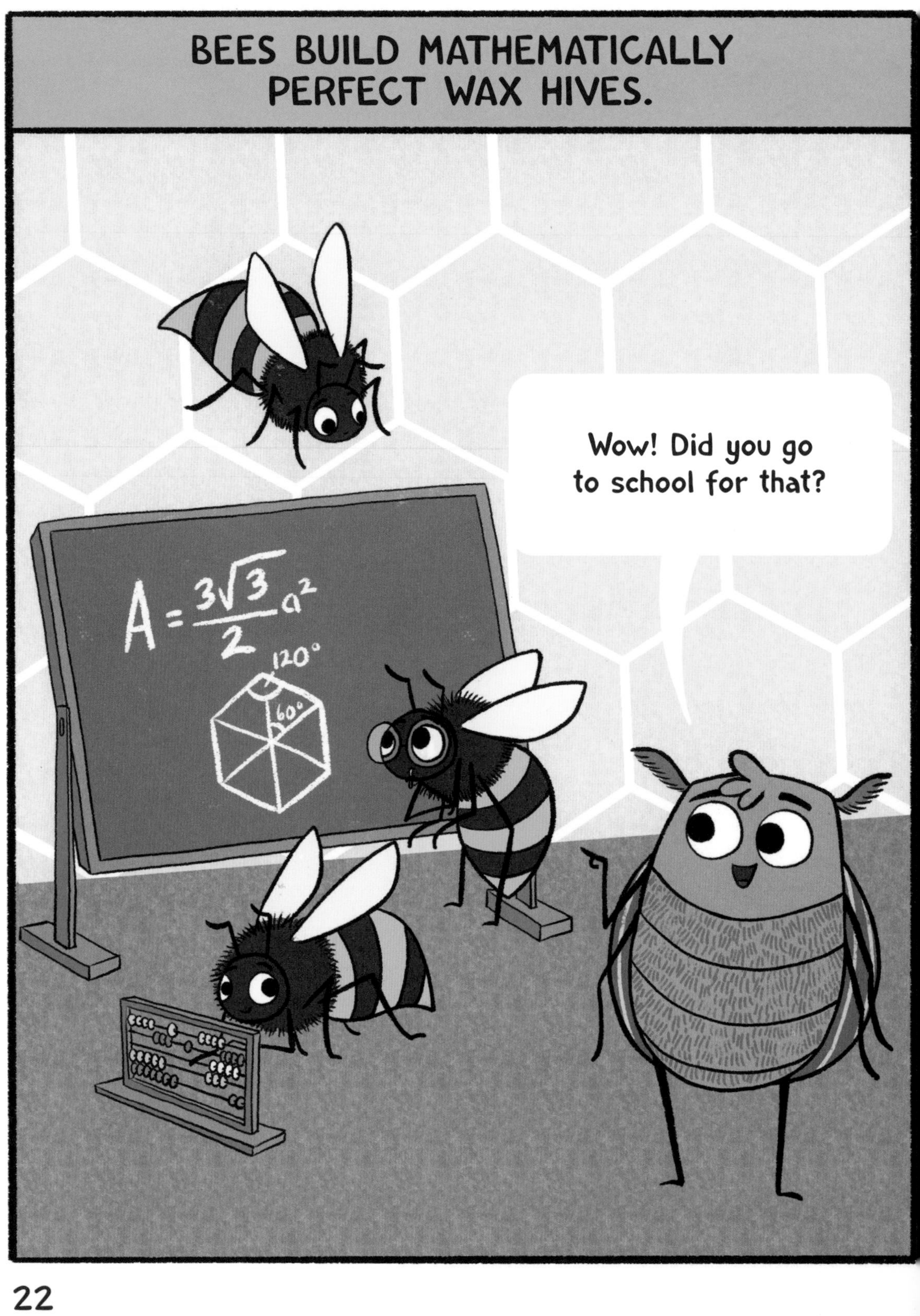
$A = \frac{3\sqrt{3}}{2}a^2$
120°
60°
Wow! Did you go to school for that?

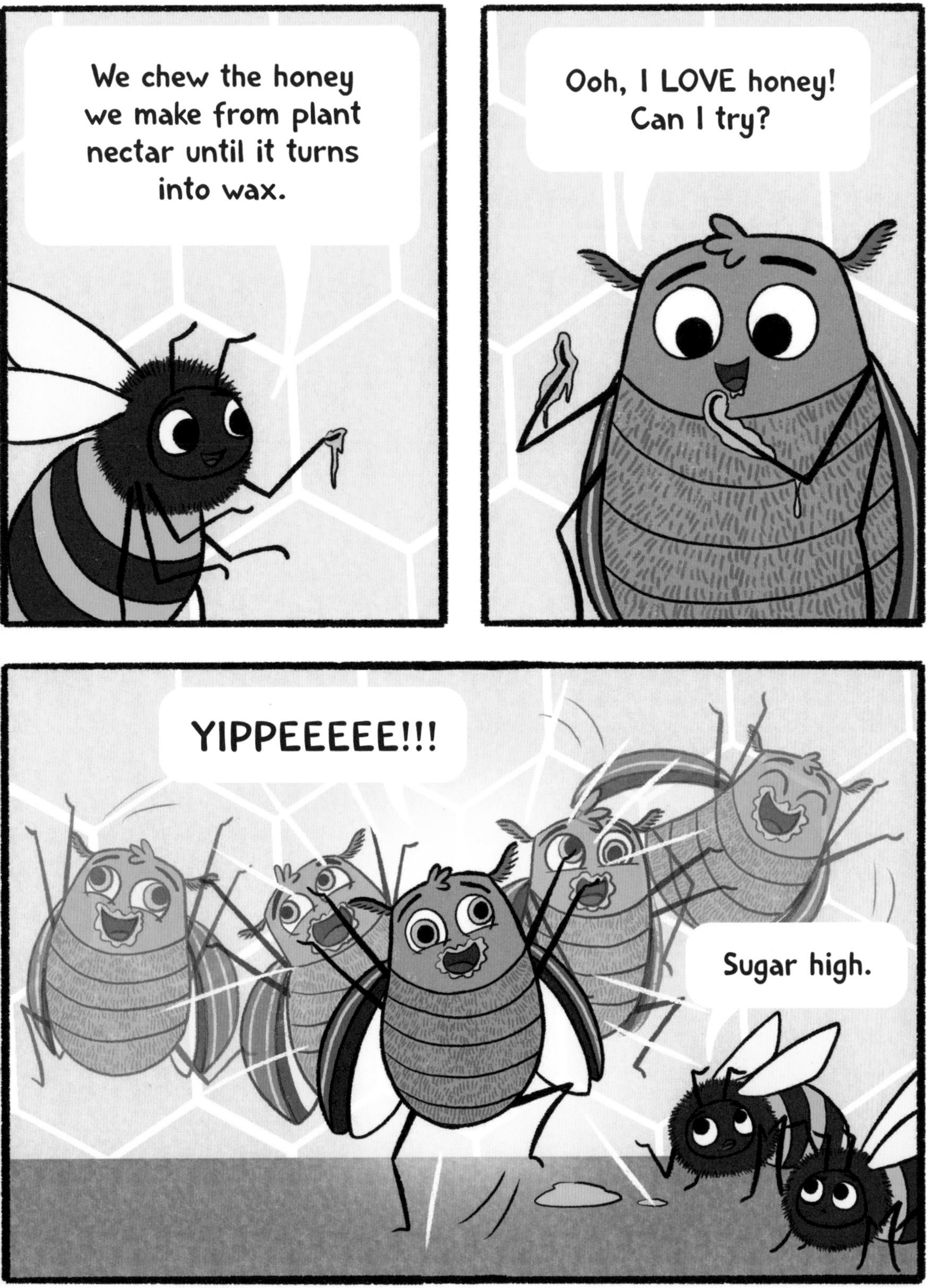
We chew the honey we make from plant nectar until it turns into wax.
Ooh, I LOVE honey! Can I try?
YIPPEEEEE!!!
Sugar high.

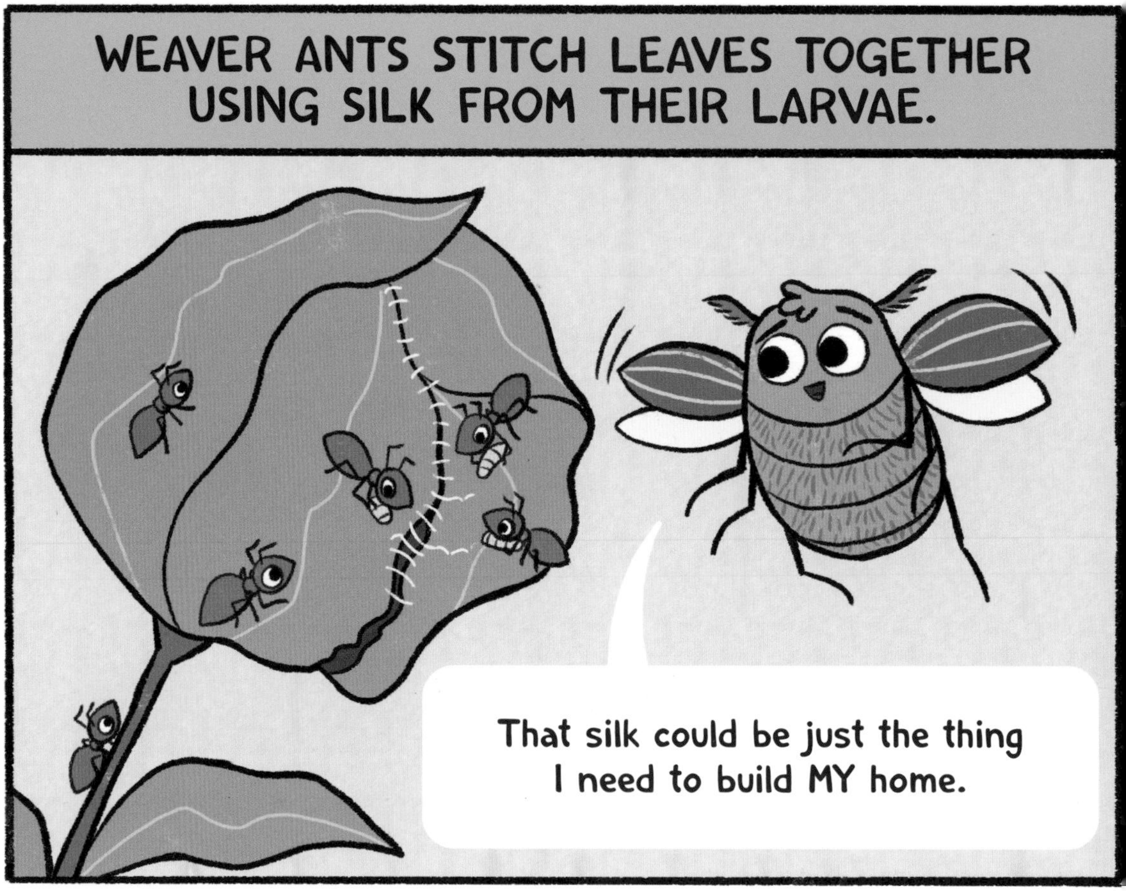
WEAVER ANTS STITCH LEAVES TOGETHER USING SILK FROM THEIR LARVAE.
That silk could be just the thing I need to build MY home.

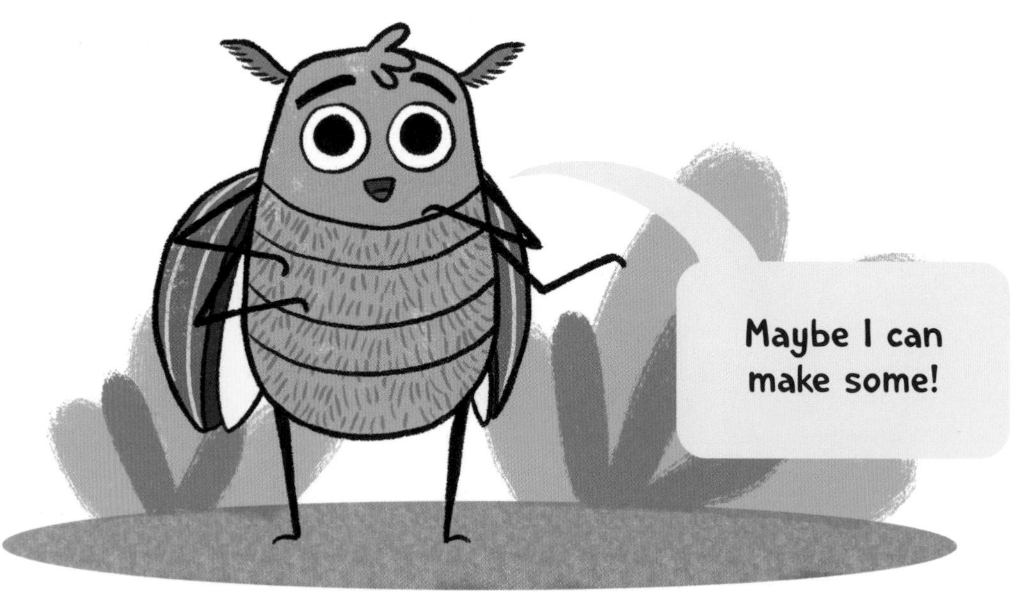
Maybe I can make some!

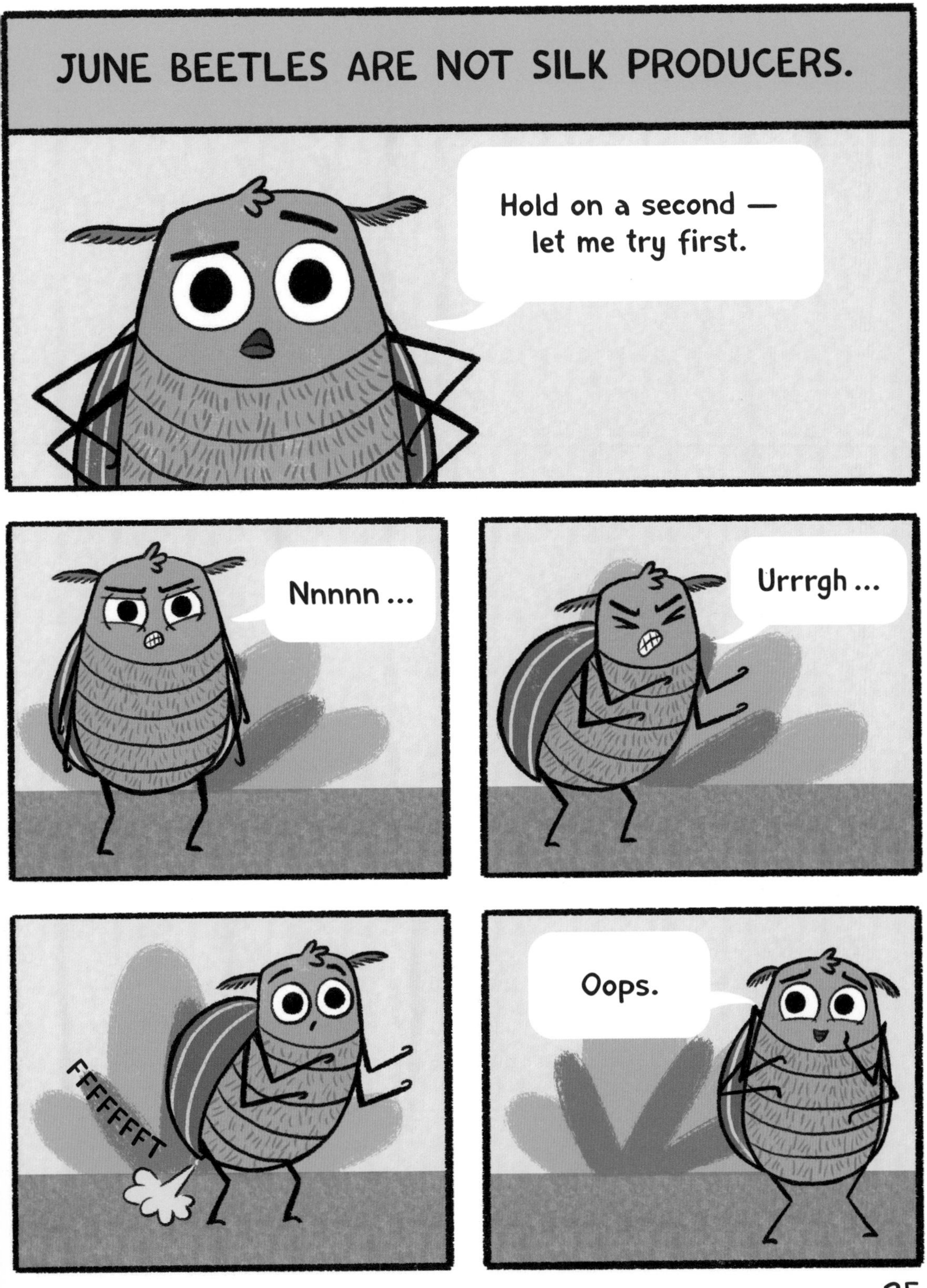
JUNE BEETLES ARE NOT SILK PRODUCERS.
Hold on a second — let me try first.
Nnnnn ...
Urrrgh ...
FFFFFFFT
Oops.

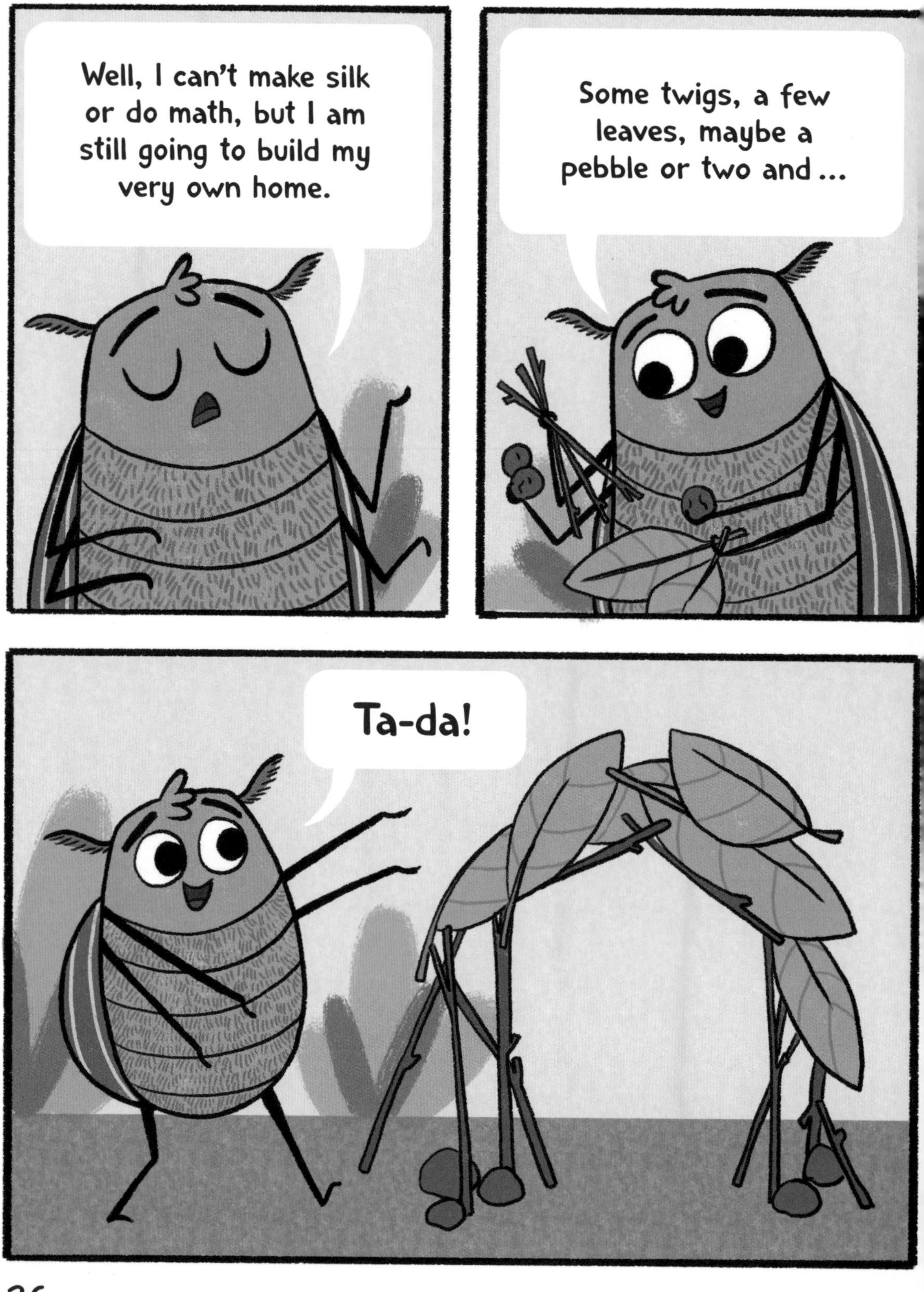
Well, I can't make silk or do math, but I am still going to build my very own home.
Some twigs, a few leaves, maybe a pebble or two and...
Ta-da!

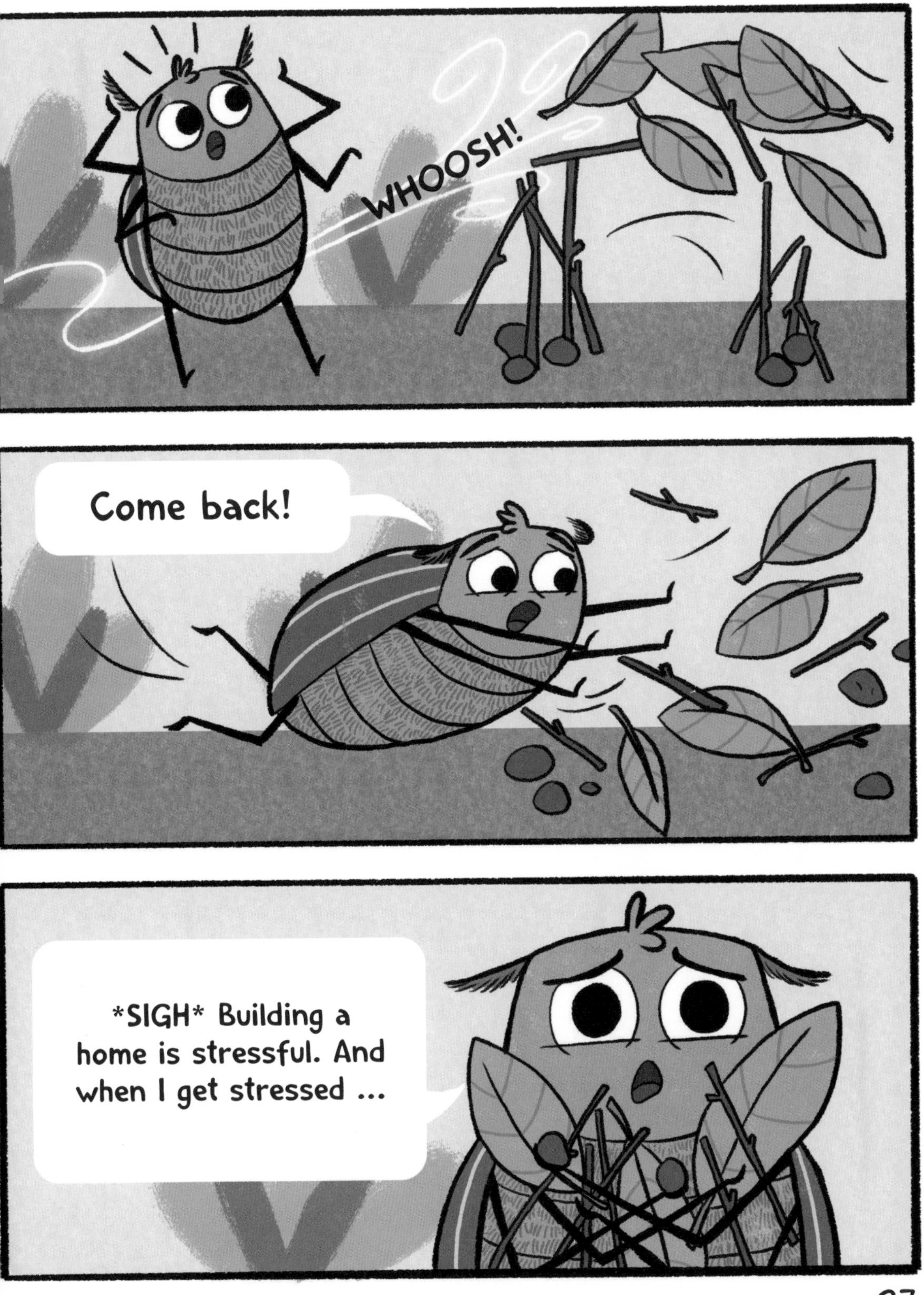
WHOOSH!
Come back!
SIGH Building a home is stressful. And when I get stressed ...

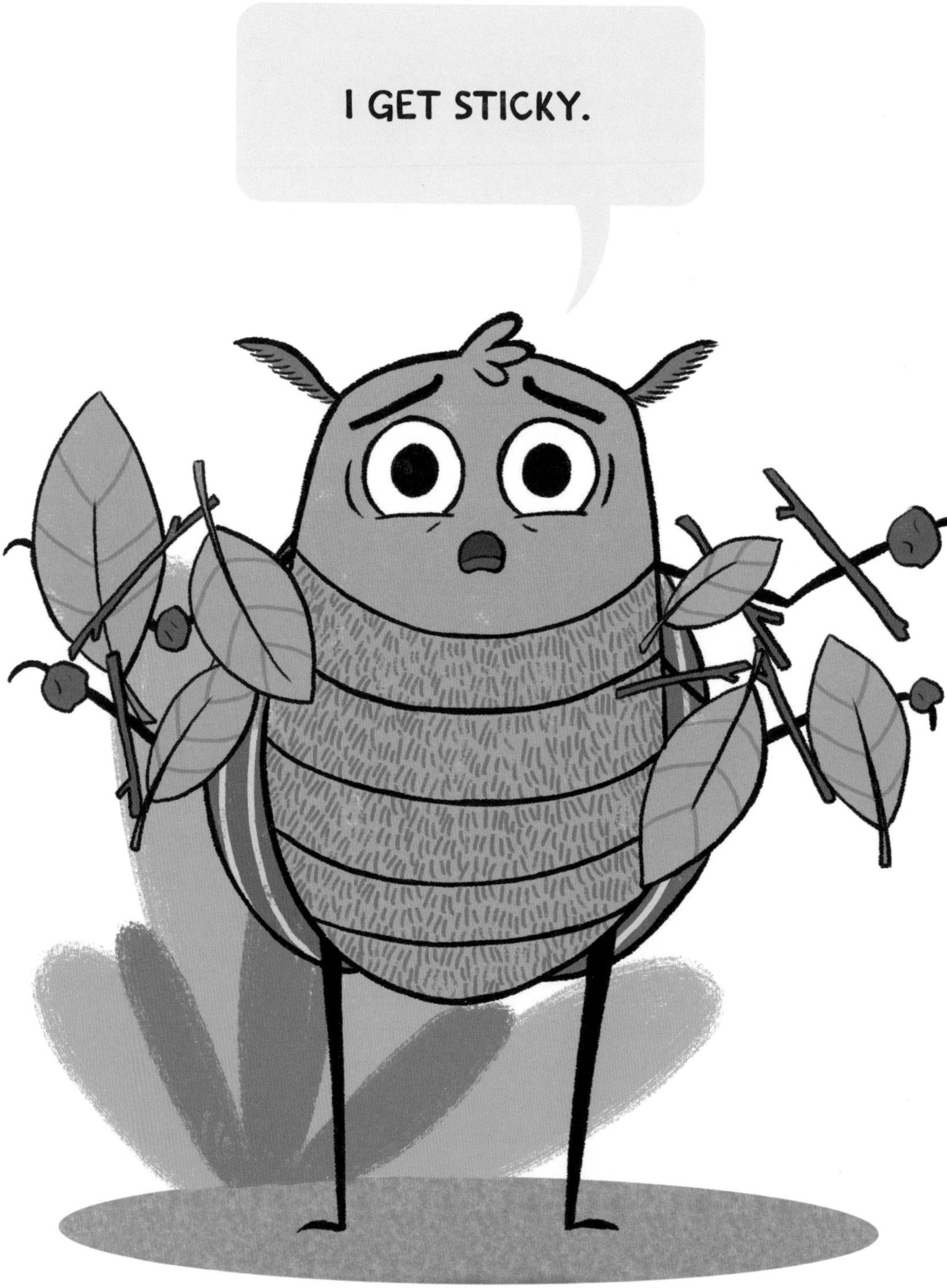
I GET STICKY.

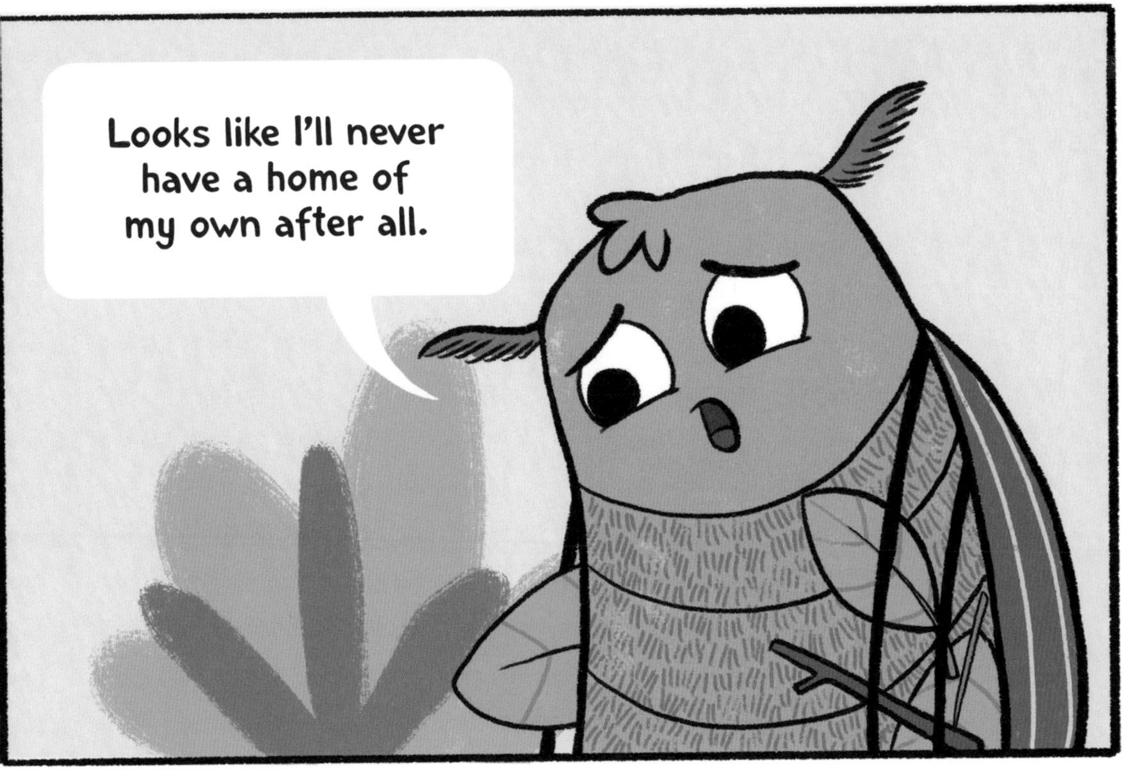
Looks like I'll never have a home of my own after all.

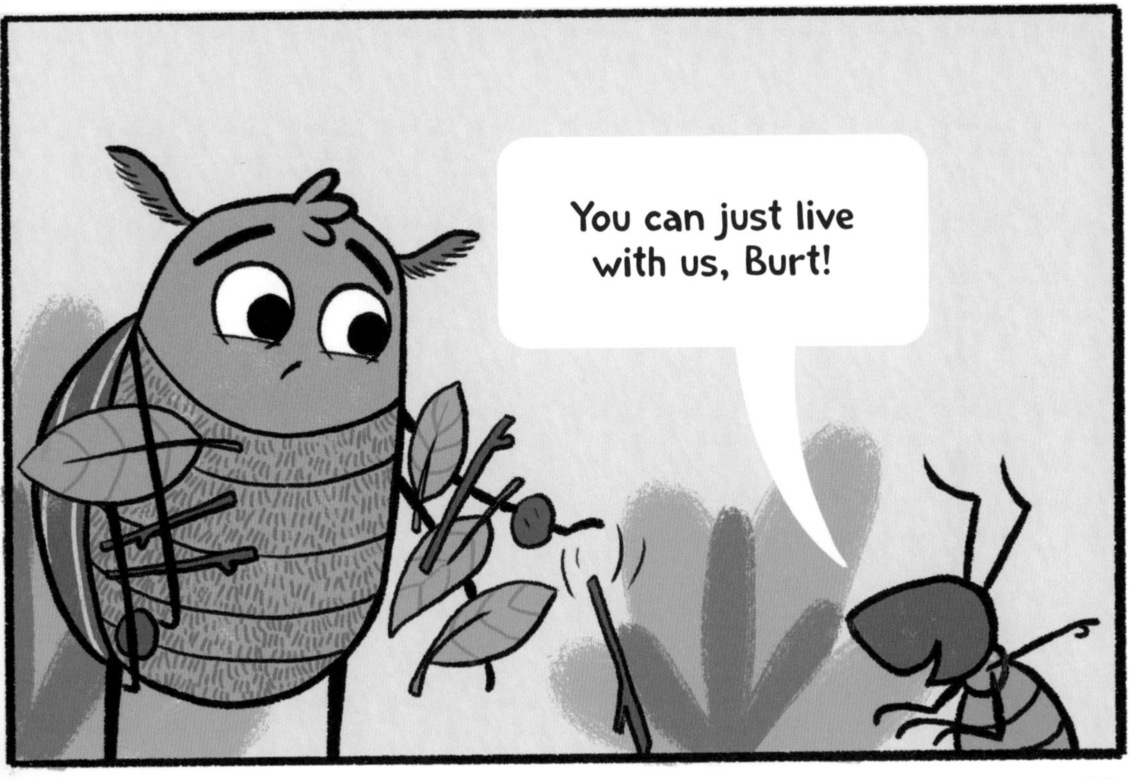
You can just live with us, Burt!

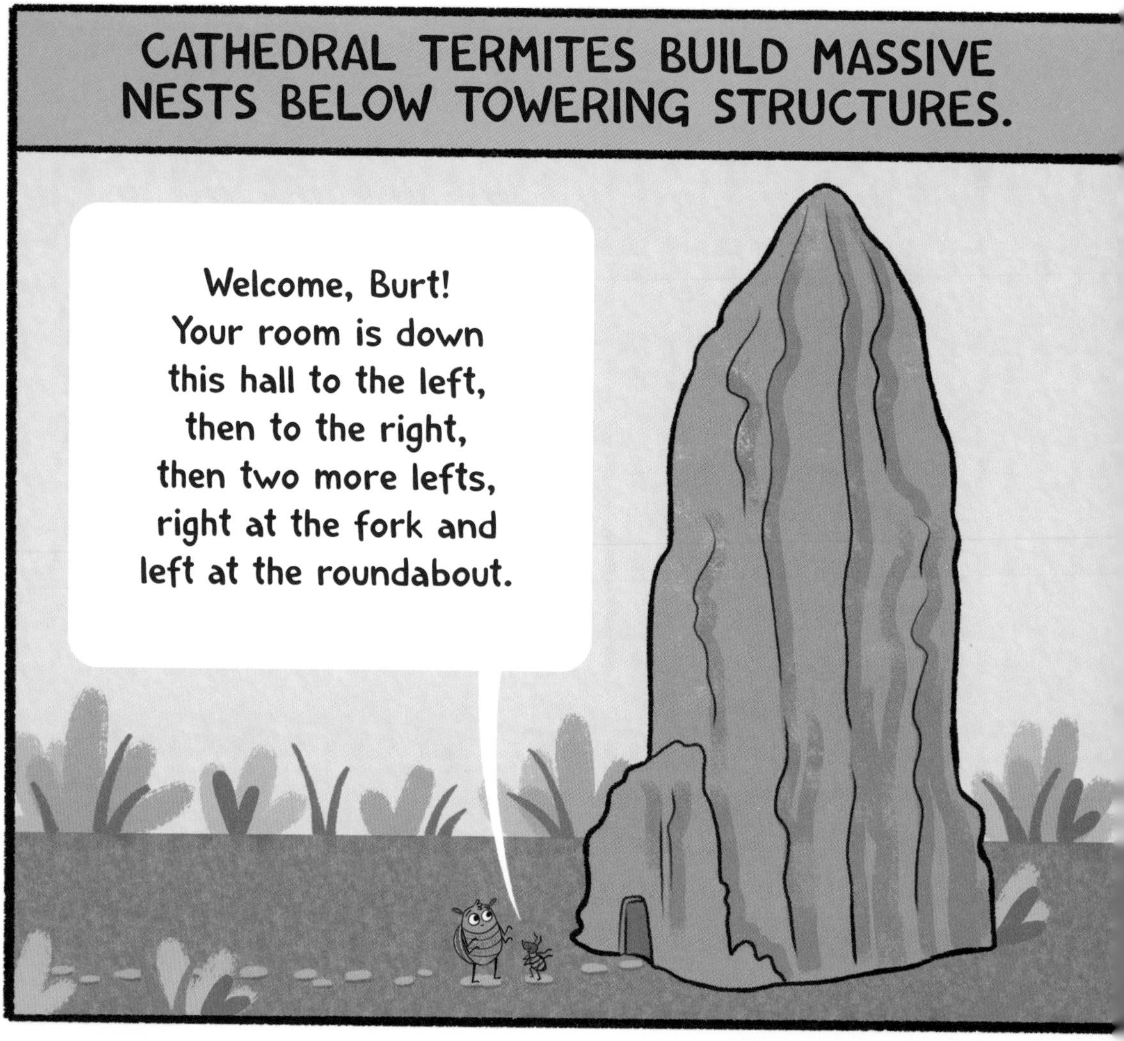
CATHEDRAL TERMITES BUILD MASSIVE NESTS BELOW TOWERING STRUCTURES.
Welcome, Burt! Your room is down this hall to the left, then to the right, then two more lefts, right at the fork and left at the roundabout.

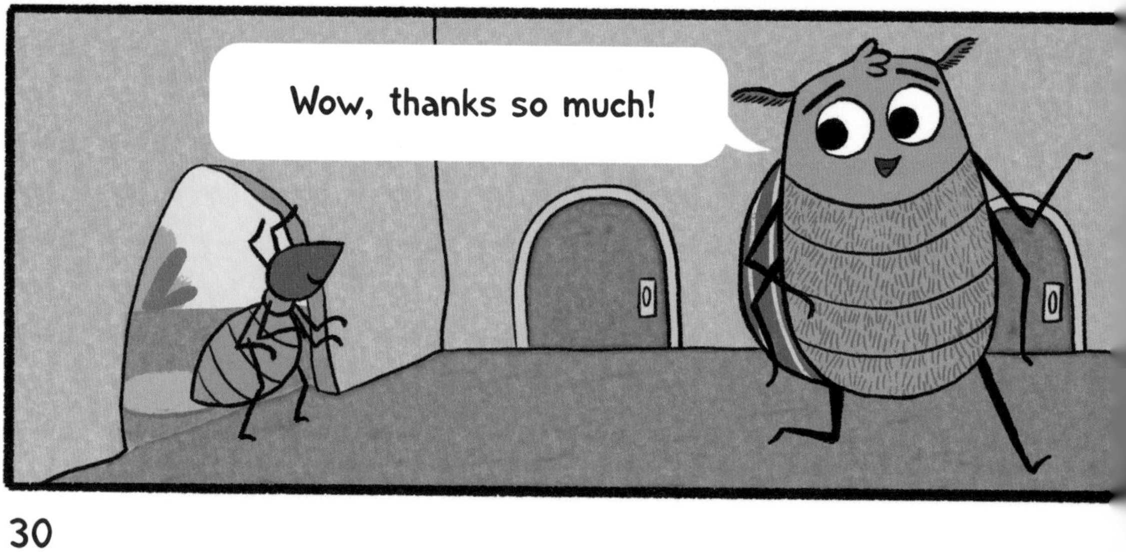
Wow, thanks so much!

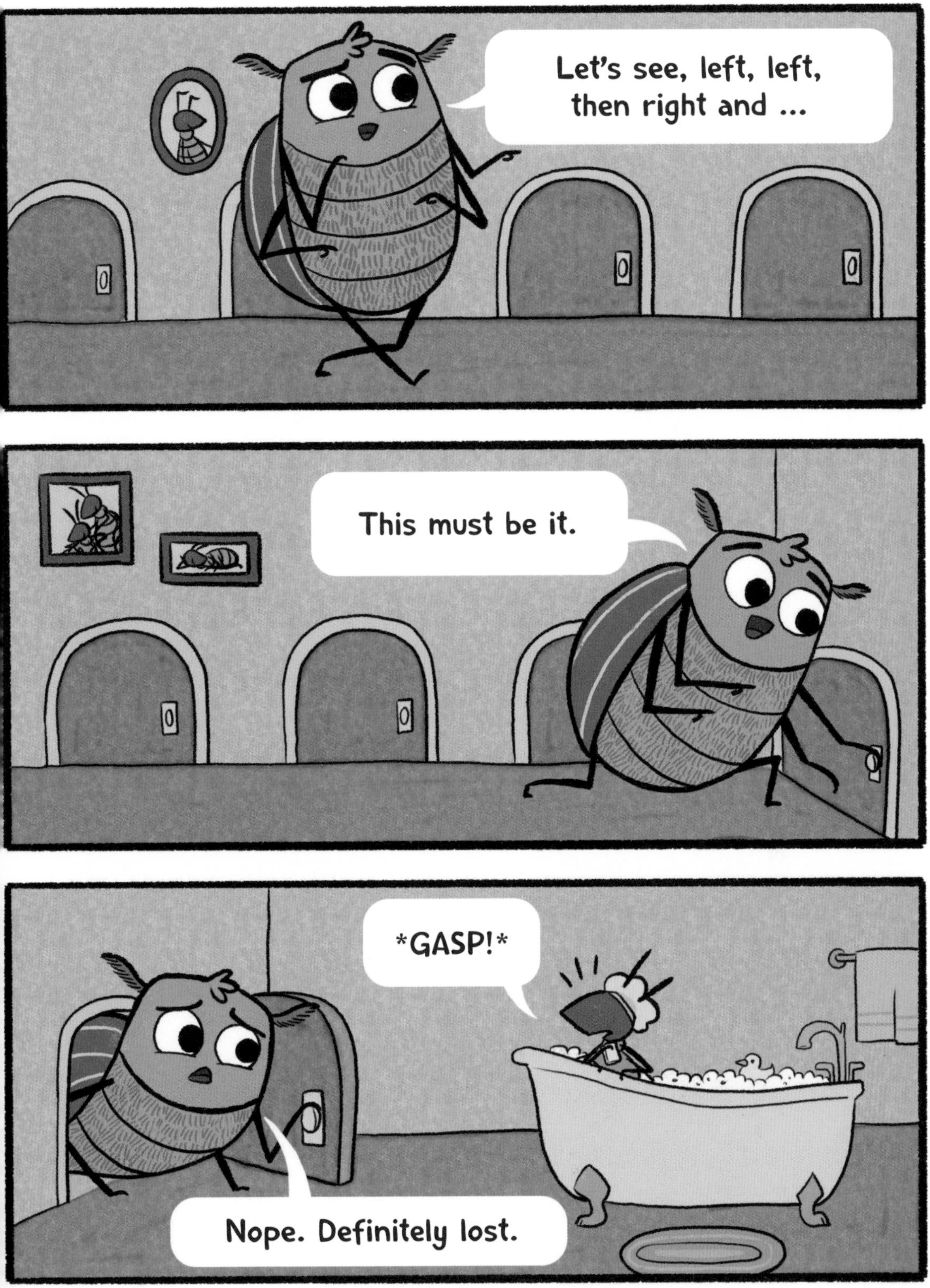
Let's see, left, left, then right and ...
This must be it.
GASP!
Nope. Definitely lost.

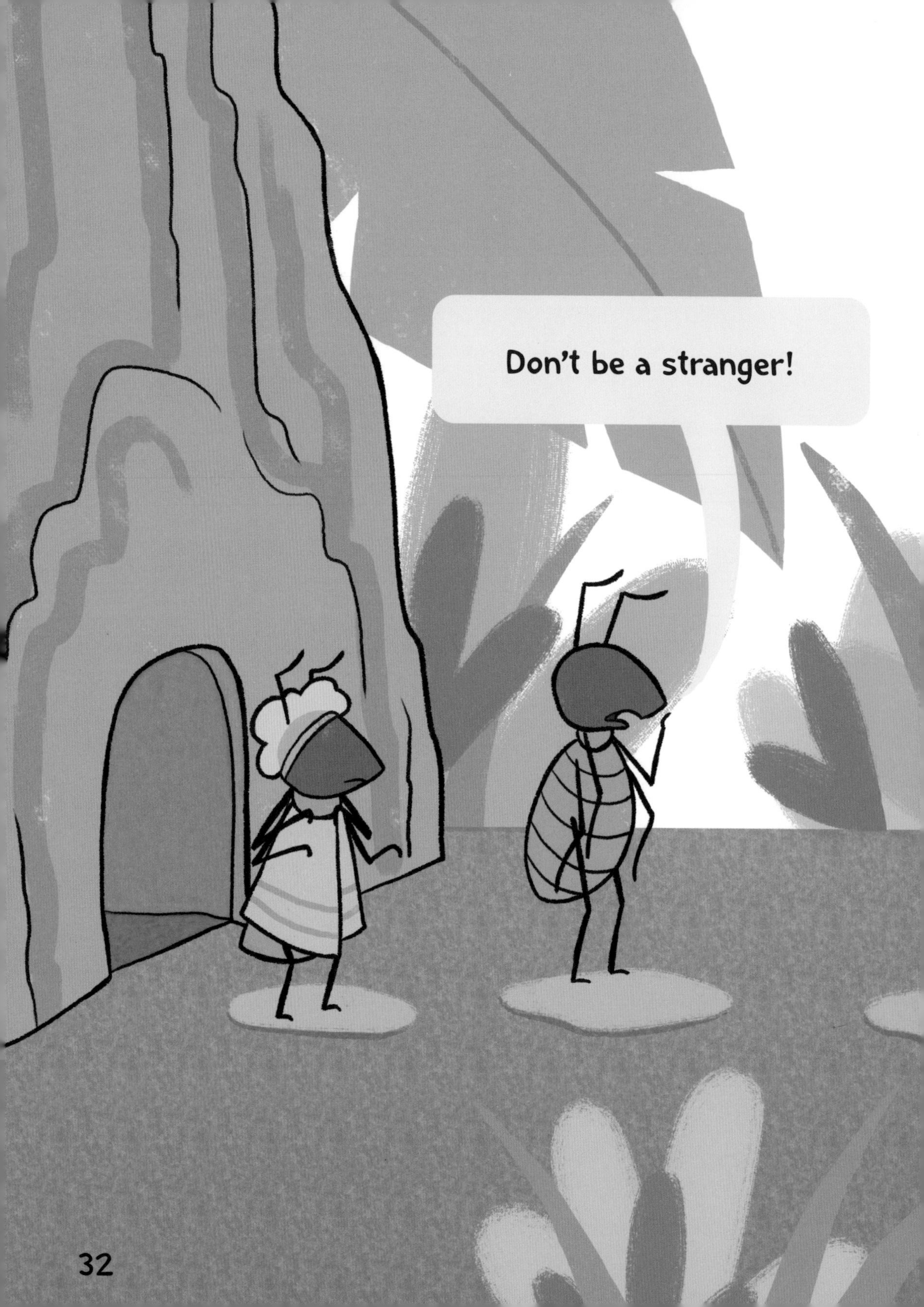
Don’t be a stranger!

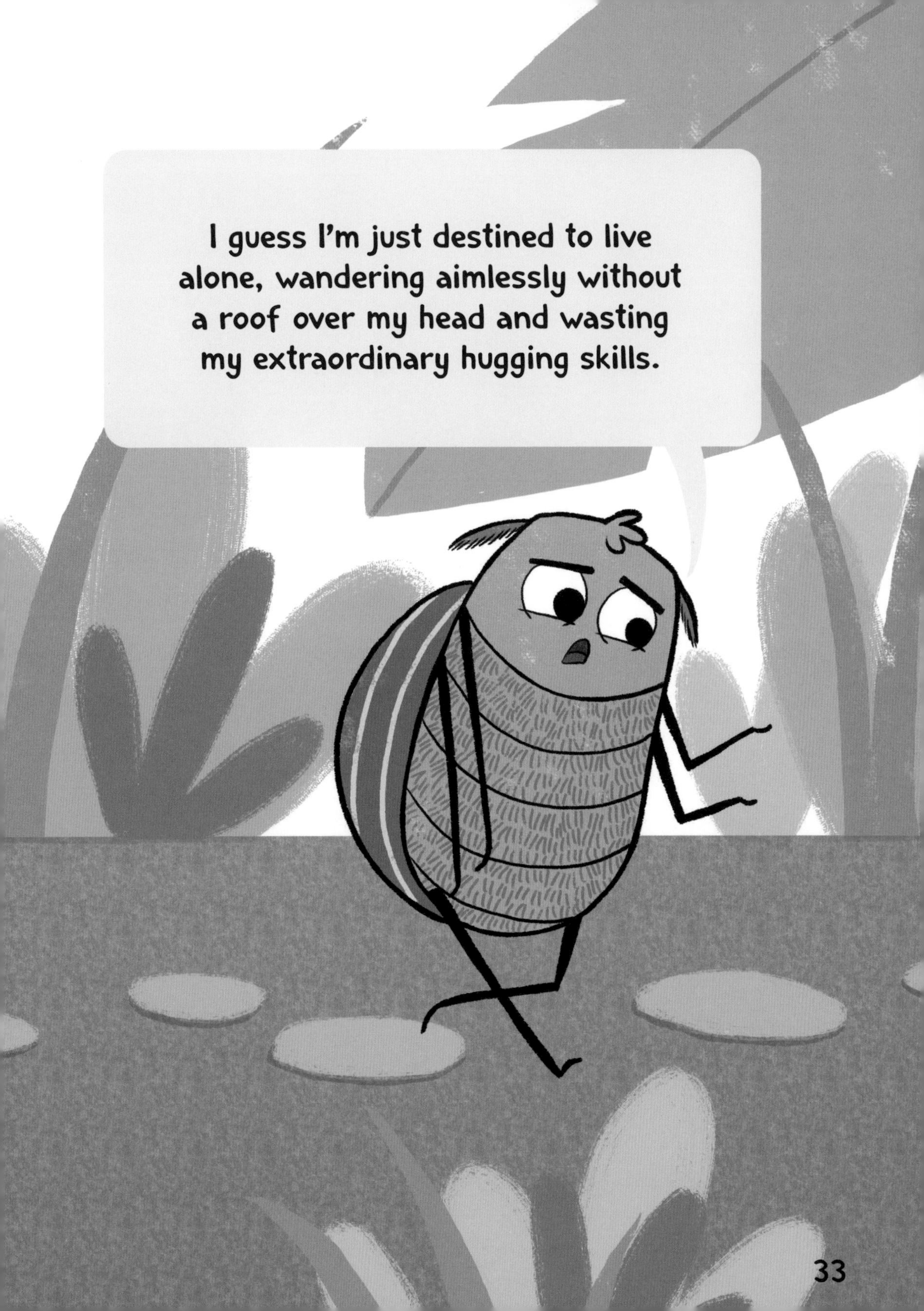
I guess I'm just destined to live alone, wandering aimlessly without a roof over my head and wasting my extraordinary hugging skills.

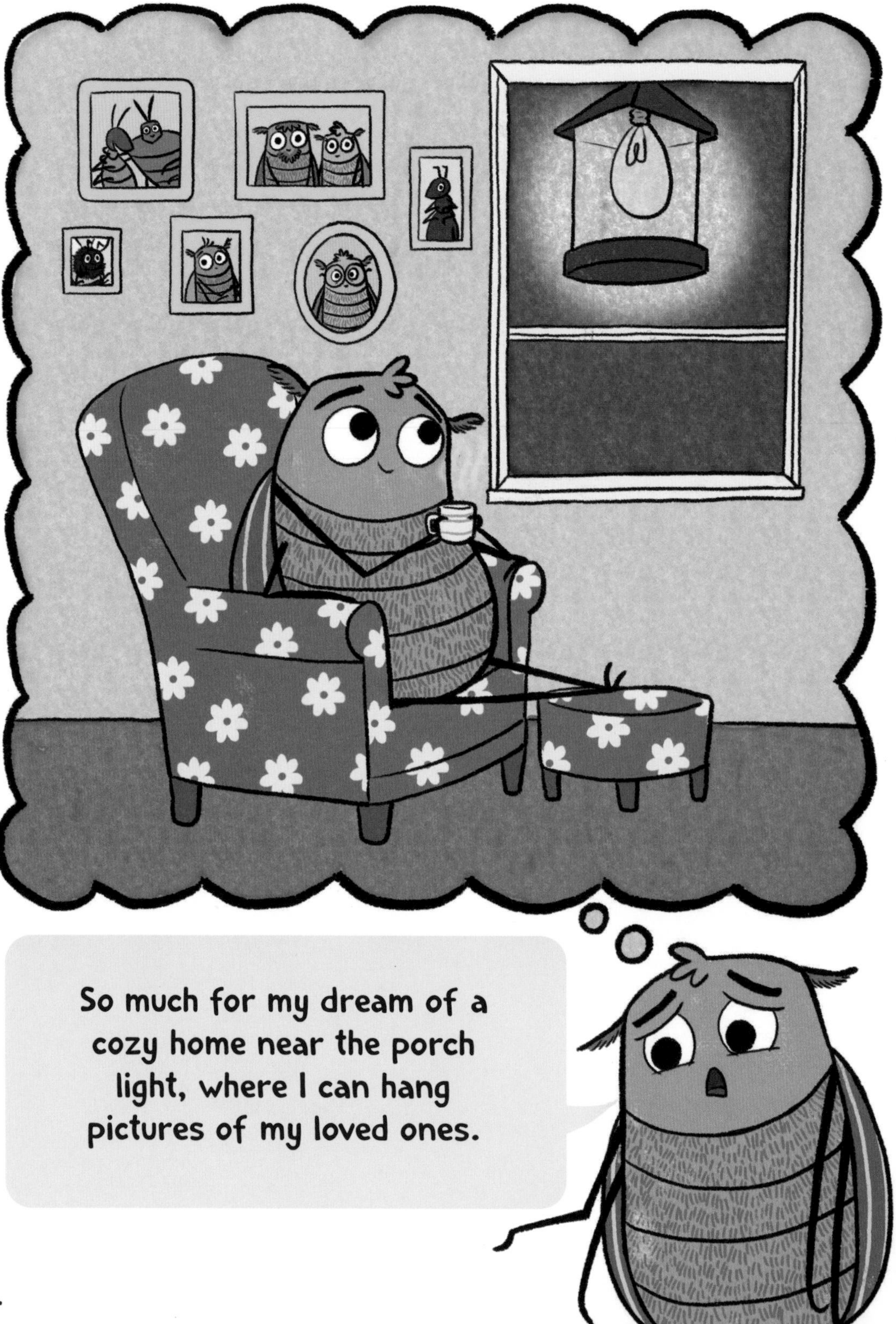
So much for my dream of a cozy home near the porch light, where I can hang pictures of my loved ones.

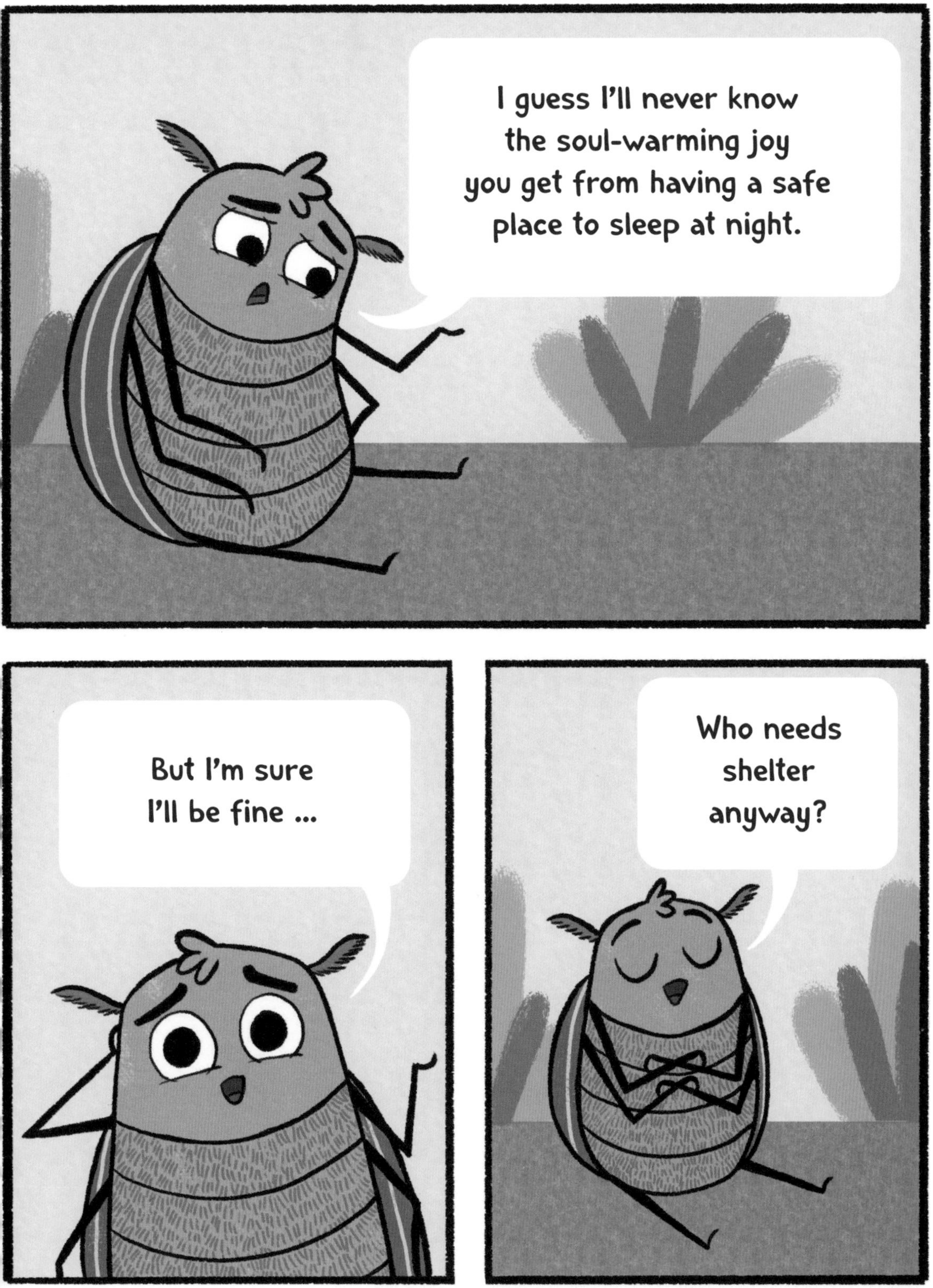
I guess I'll never know the soul-warming joy you get from having a safe place to sleep at night.
But I'm sure I'll be fine ...
Who needs shelter anyway?

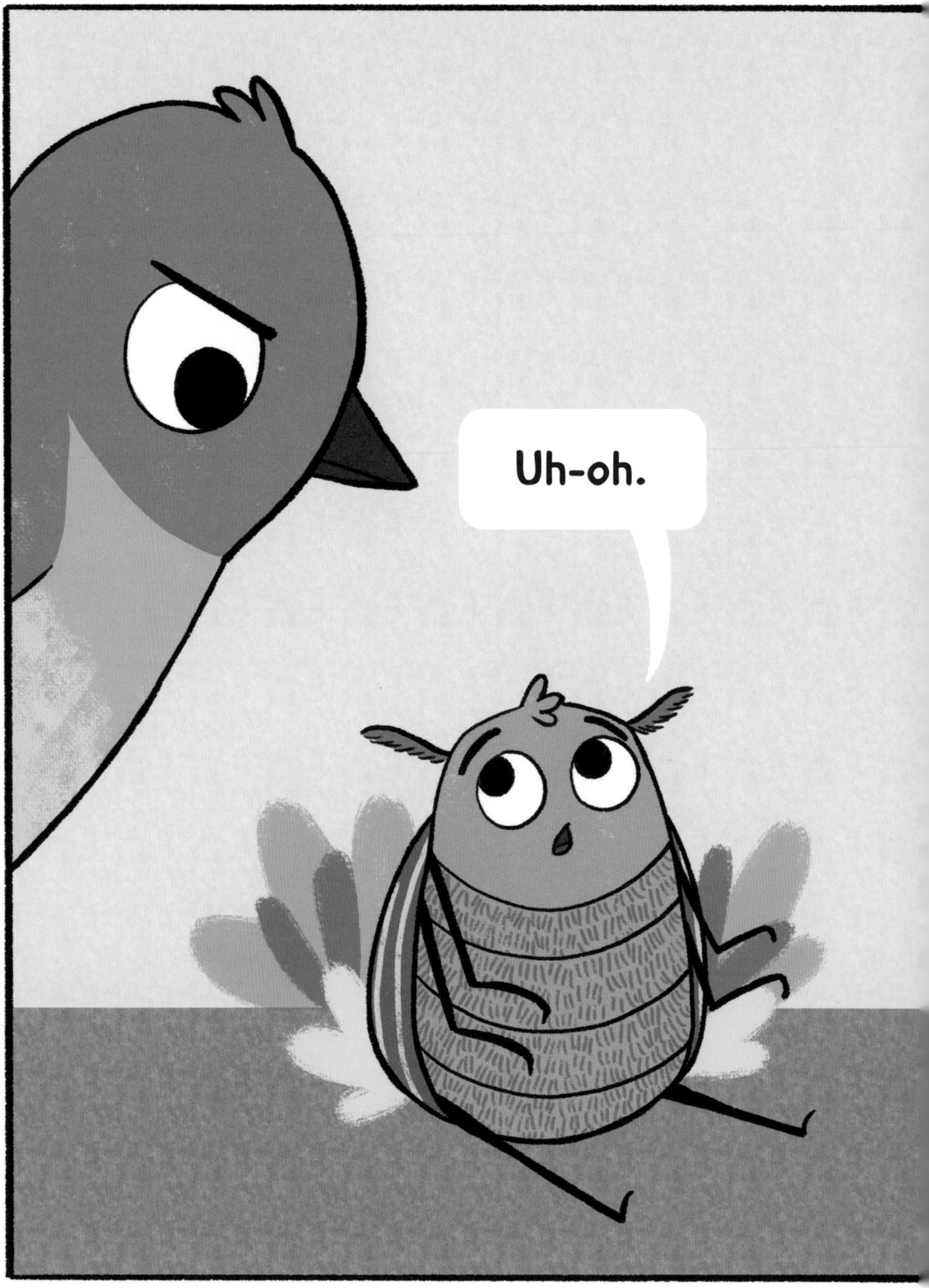
Uh-oh.

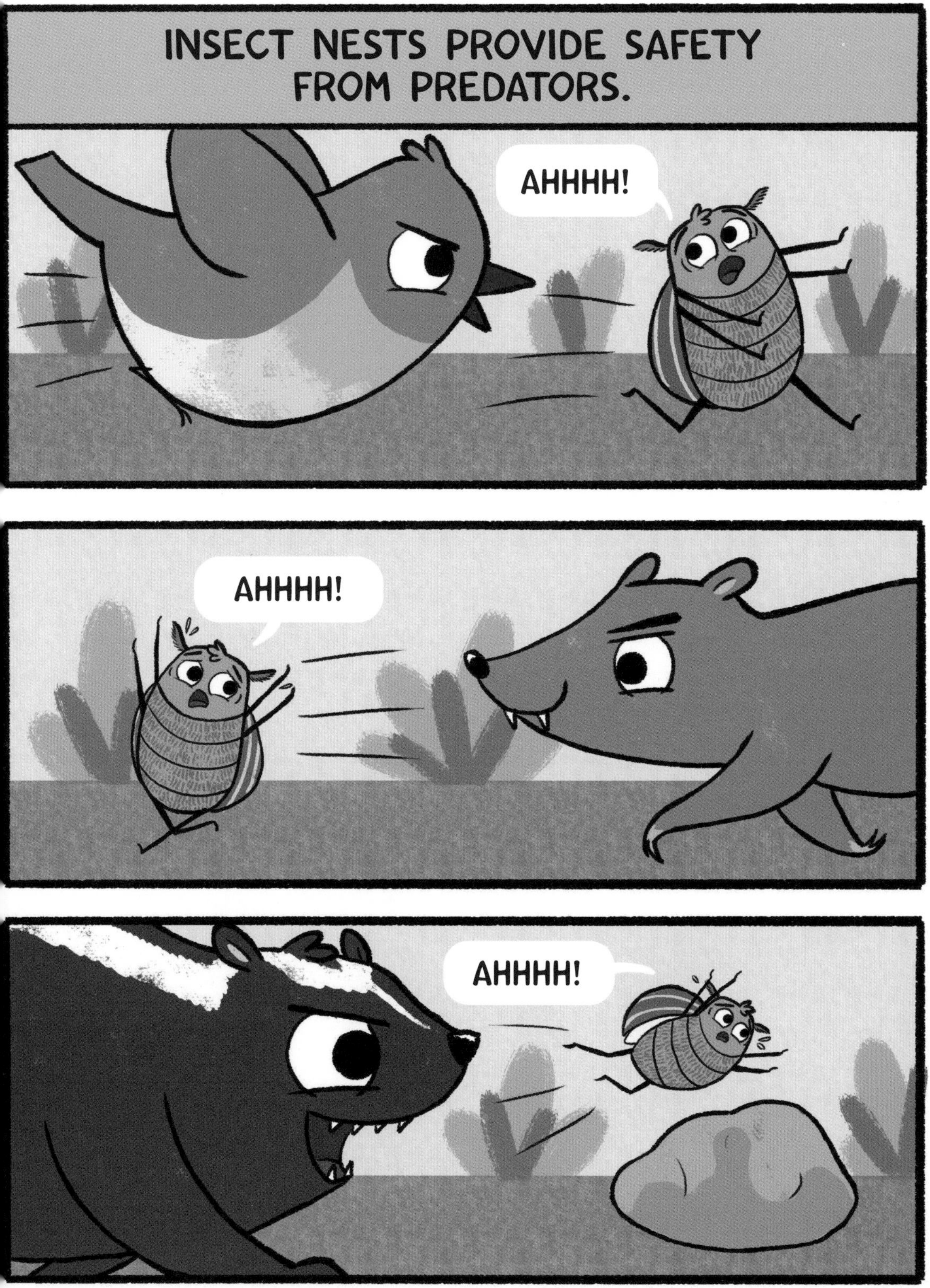
INSECT NESTS PROVIDE SAFETY FROM PREDATORS.
AHHHH!
AHHHH!
AHHHH!

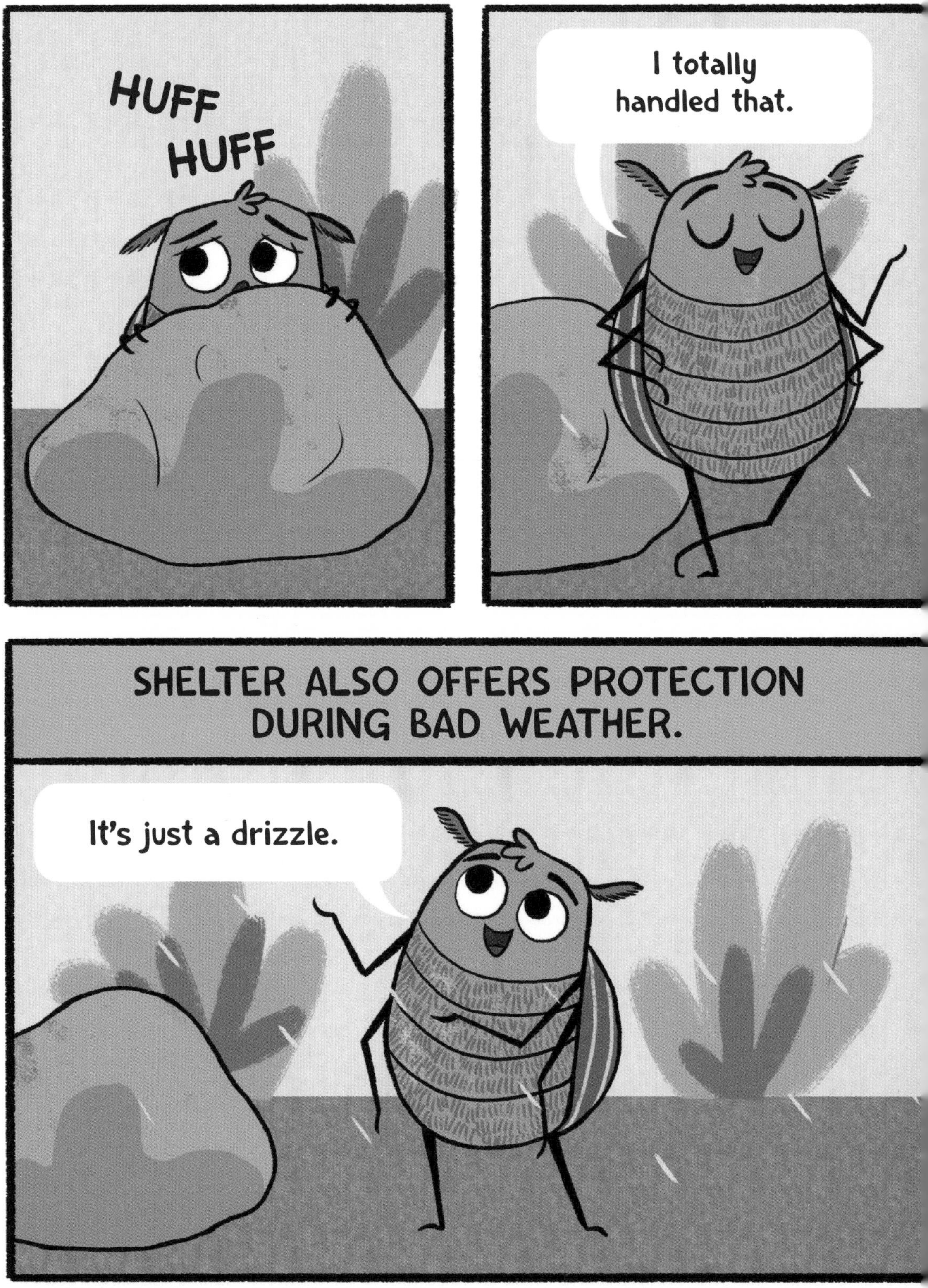
HUFF
HUFF
I totally handled that.
SHELTER ALSO OFFERS PROTECTION DURING BAD WEATHER.
It's just a drizzle.

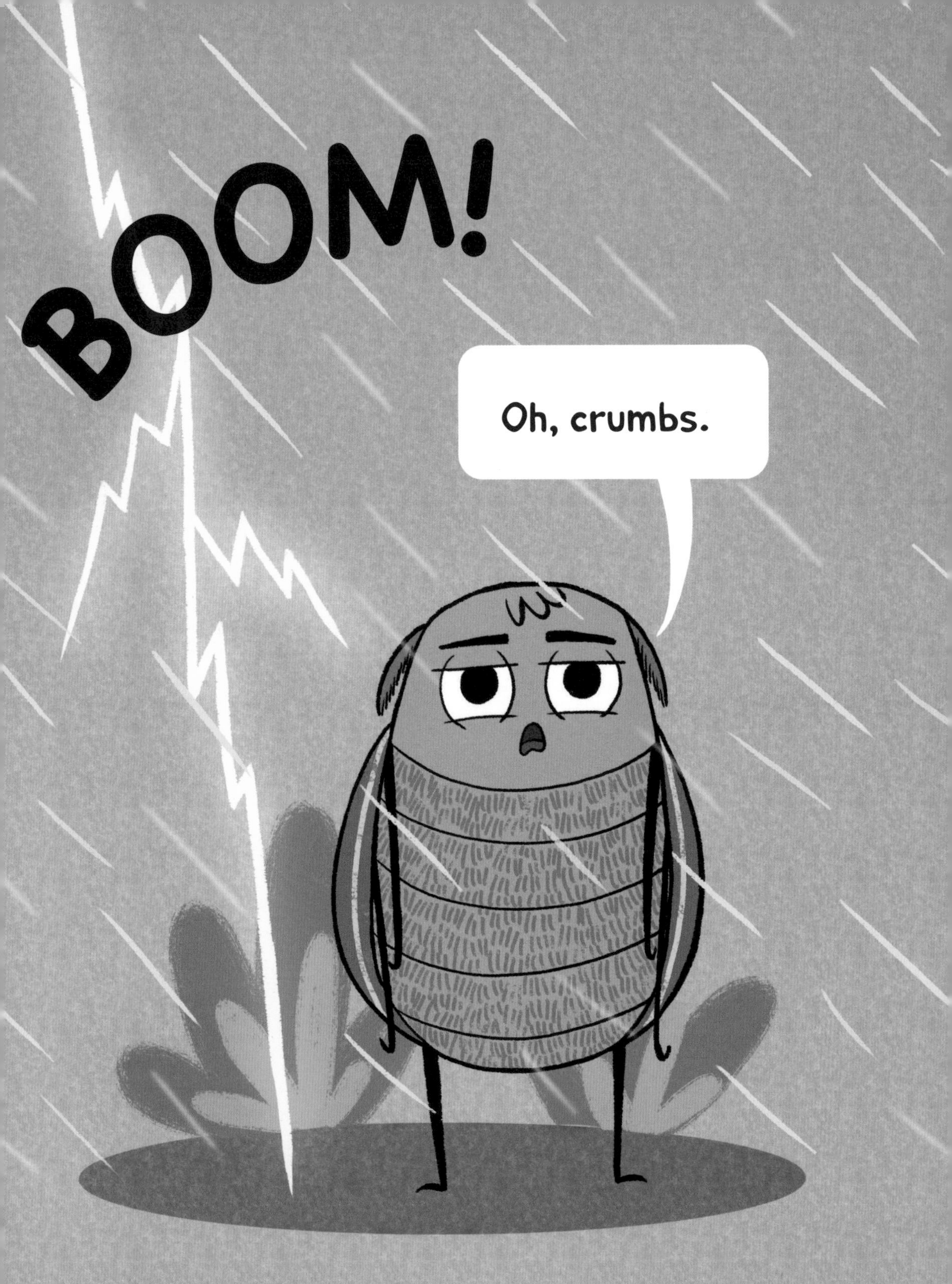
BOOM!
Oh, crumbs.

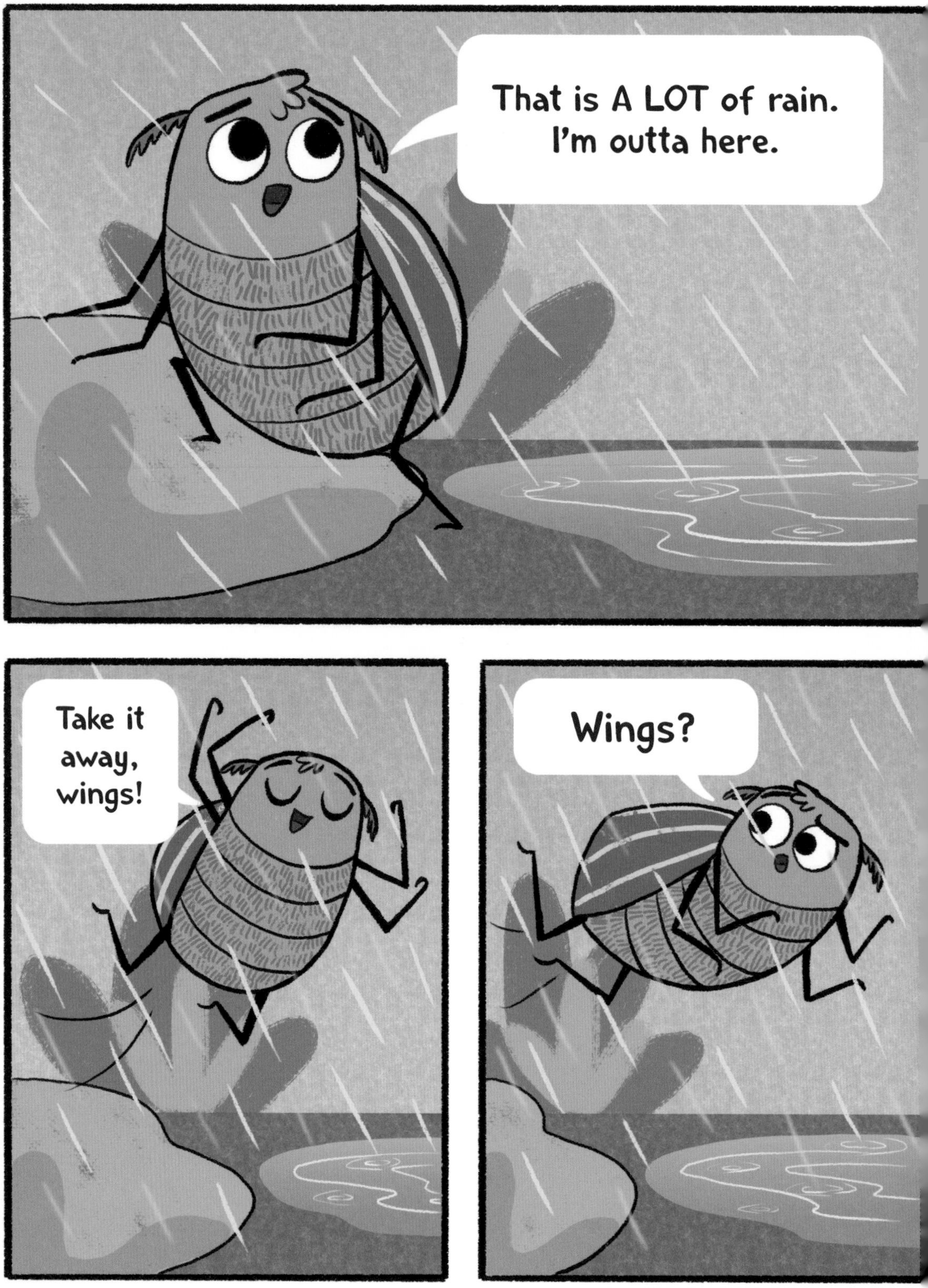
That is A LOT of rain. I'm outta here.
Take it away, wings!
Wings?

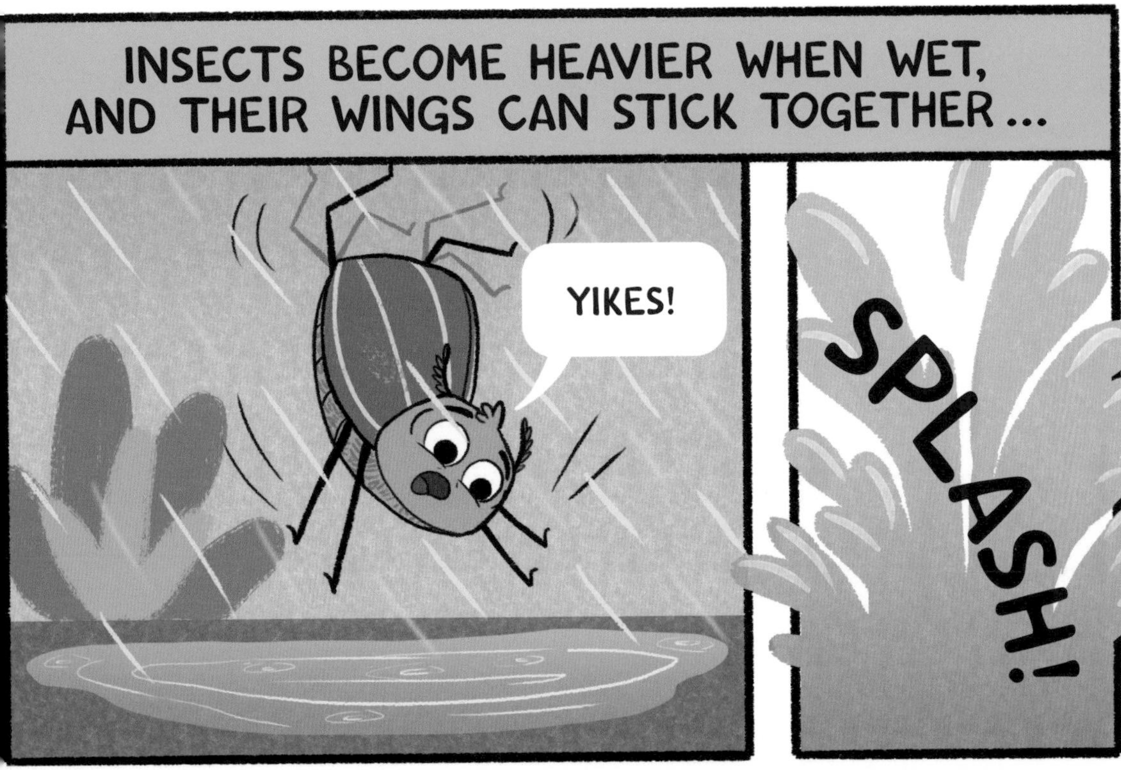
INSECTS BECOME HEAVIER WHEN WET, AND THEIR WINGS CAN STICK TOGETHER...
YIKES!
SPLASH!

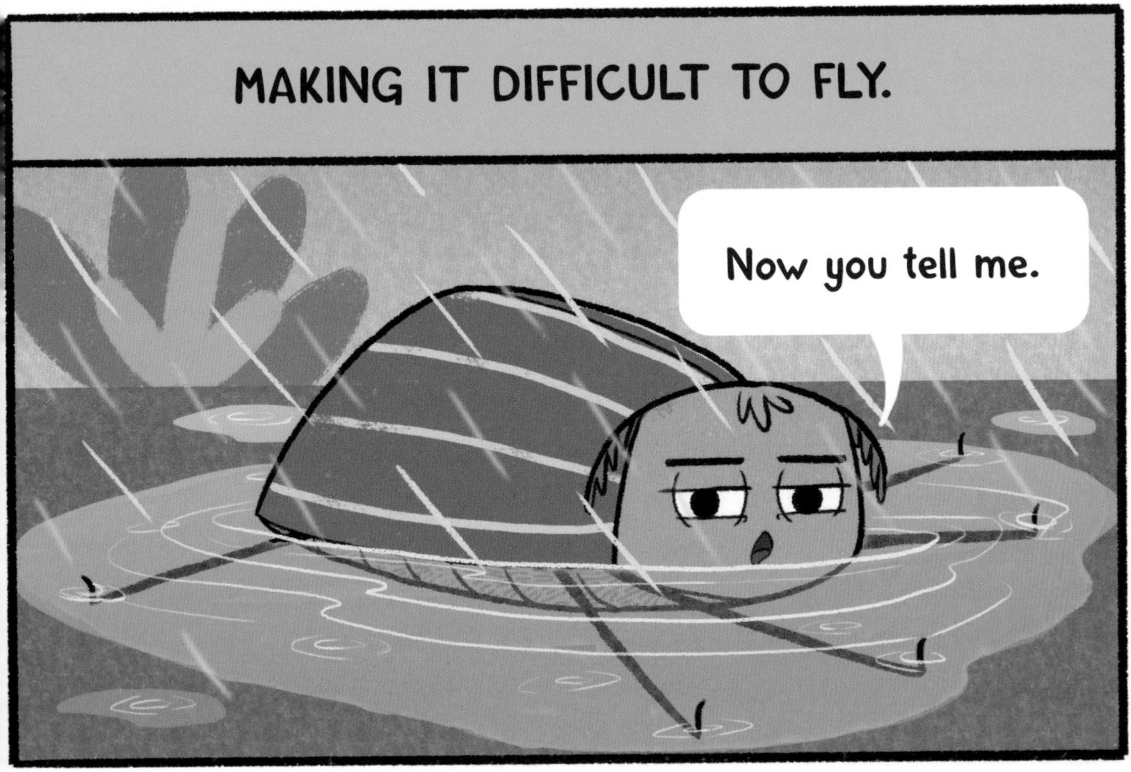
MAKING IT DIFFICULT TO FLY.
Now you tell me.

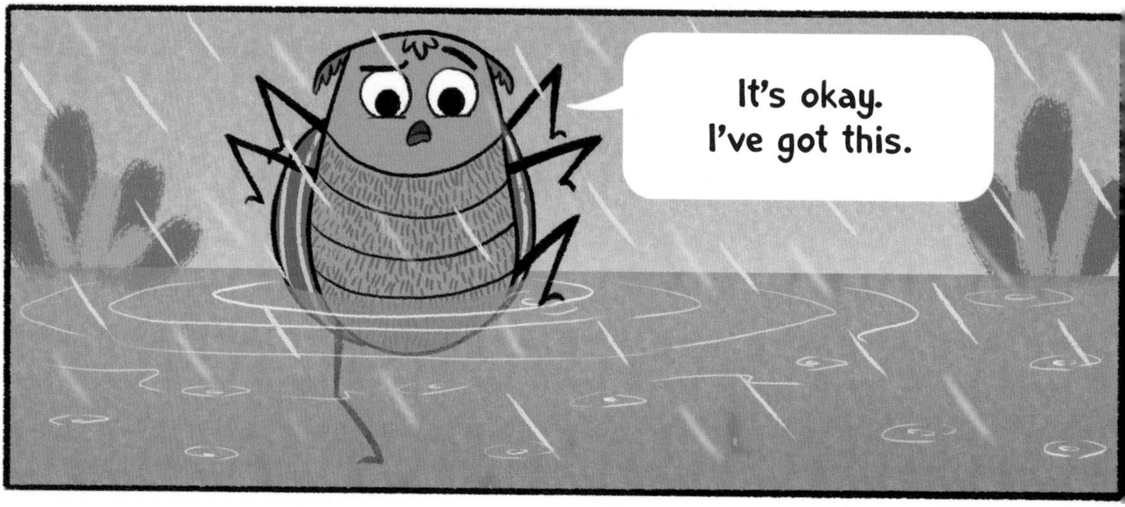
It's okay.
I've got this.

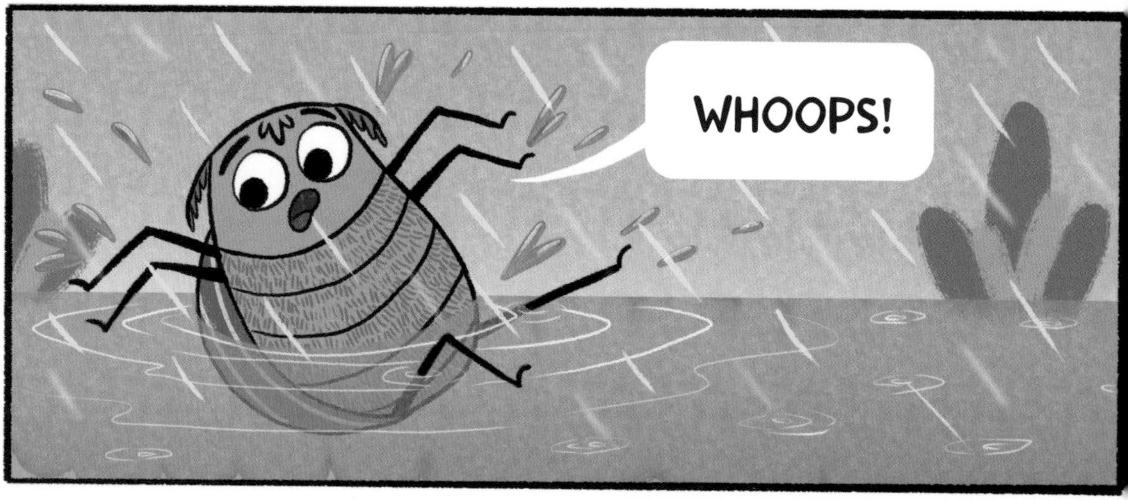
WHOOPS!

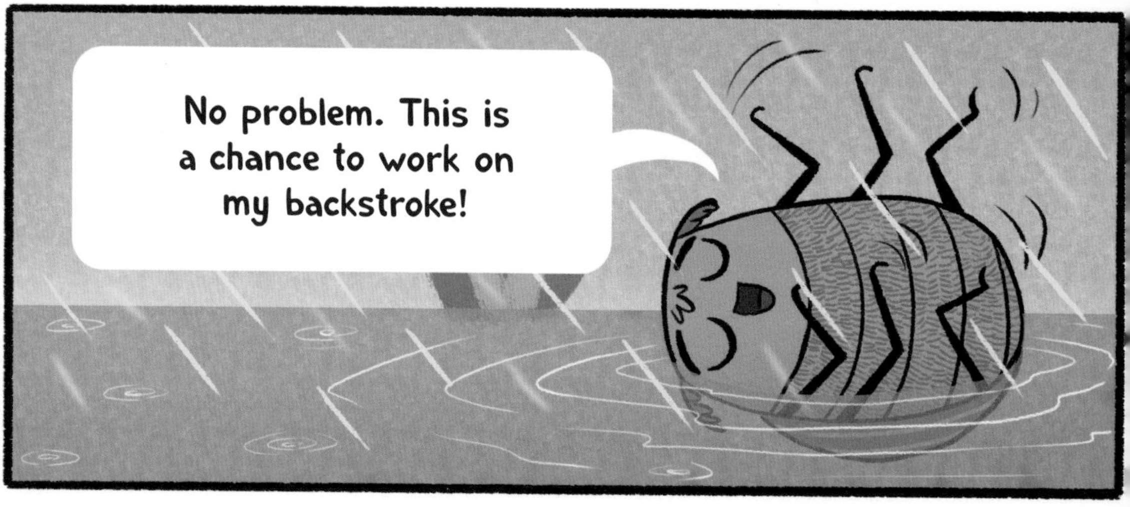
No problem. This is a chance to work on my backstroke!

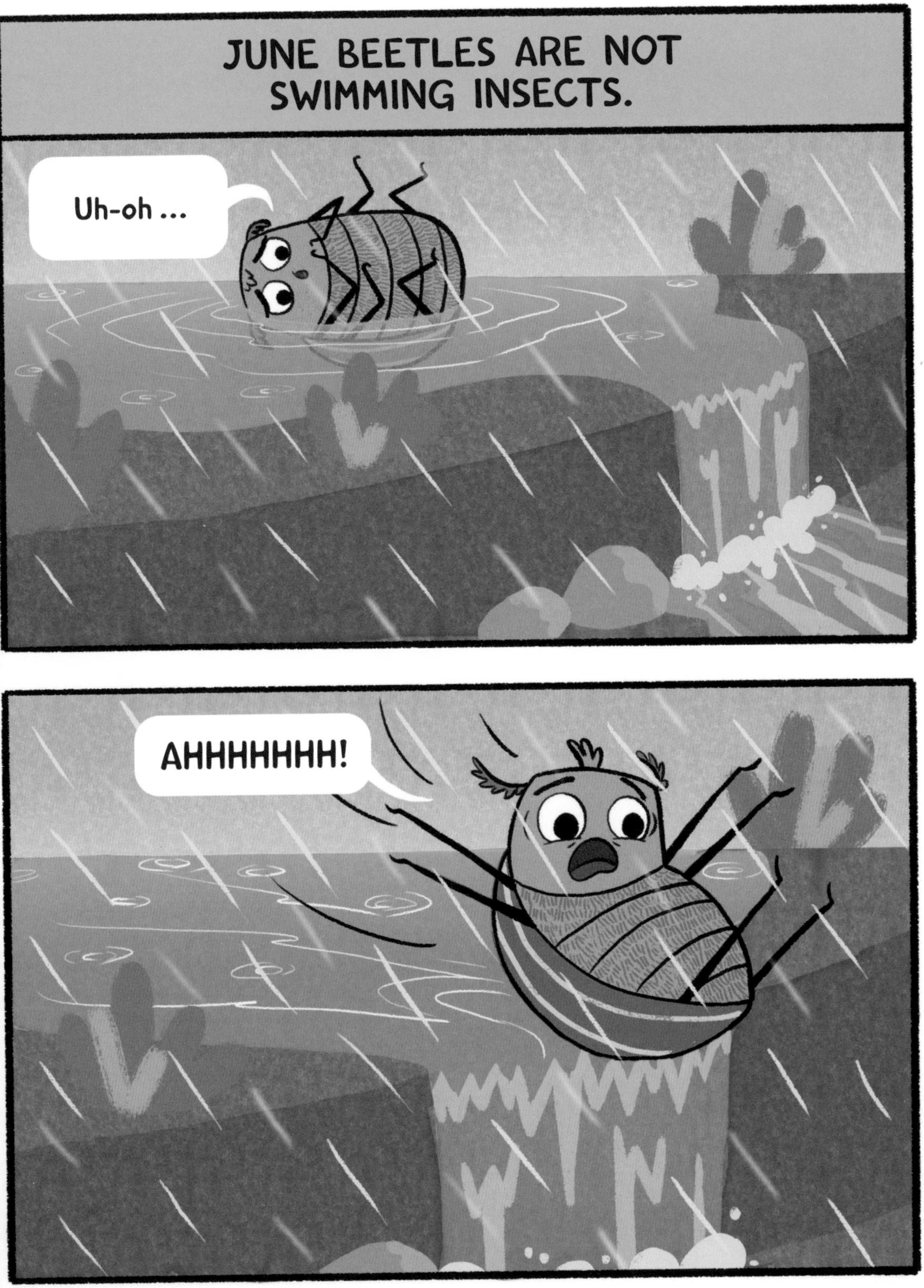
JUNE BEETLES ARE NOT SWIMMING INSECTS.
Uh-oh ...
AHHHHHHH!

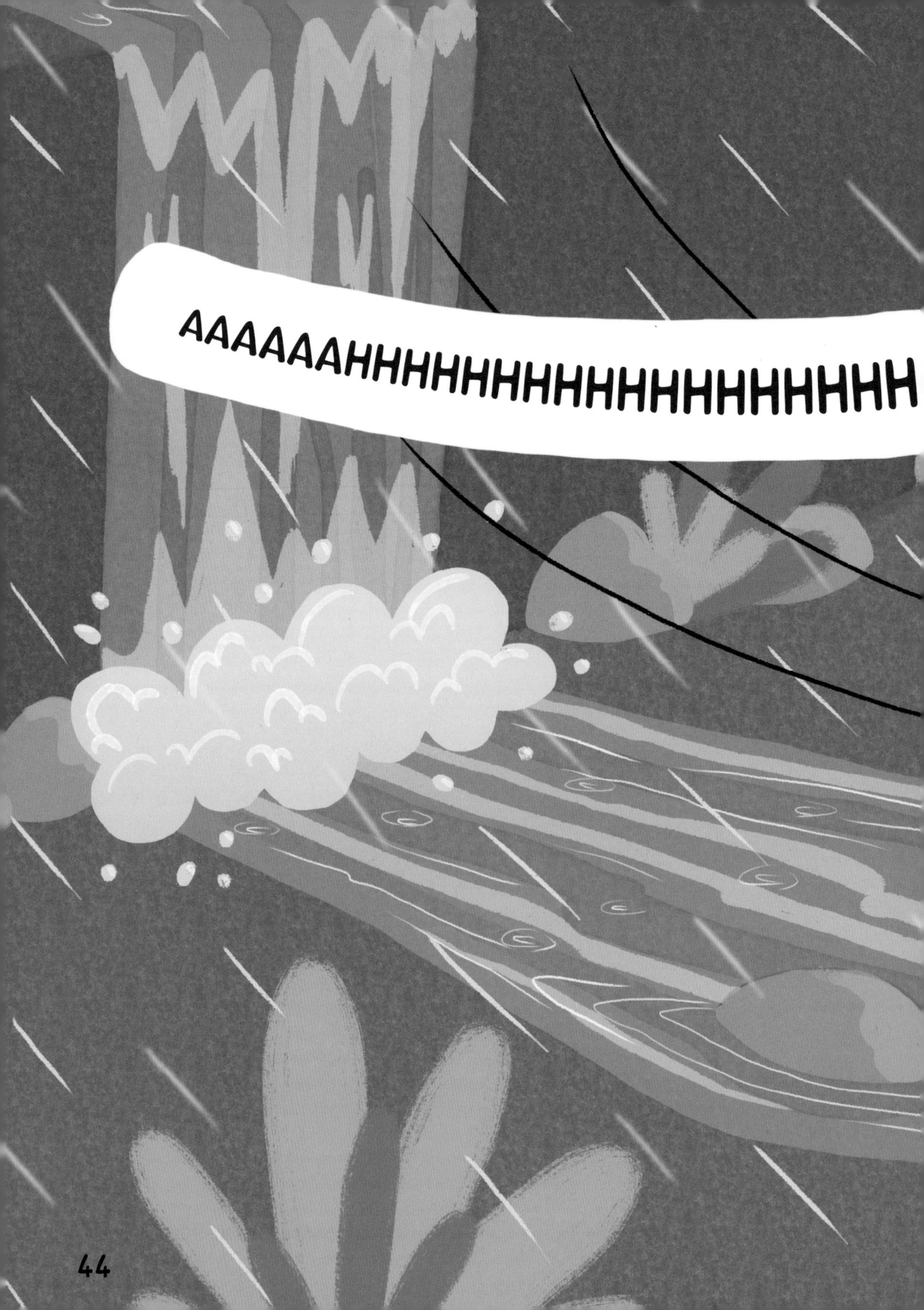
AAAAAAHHHHHHHHHHHHHHHHHHH

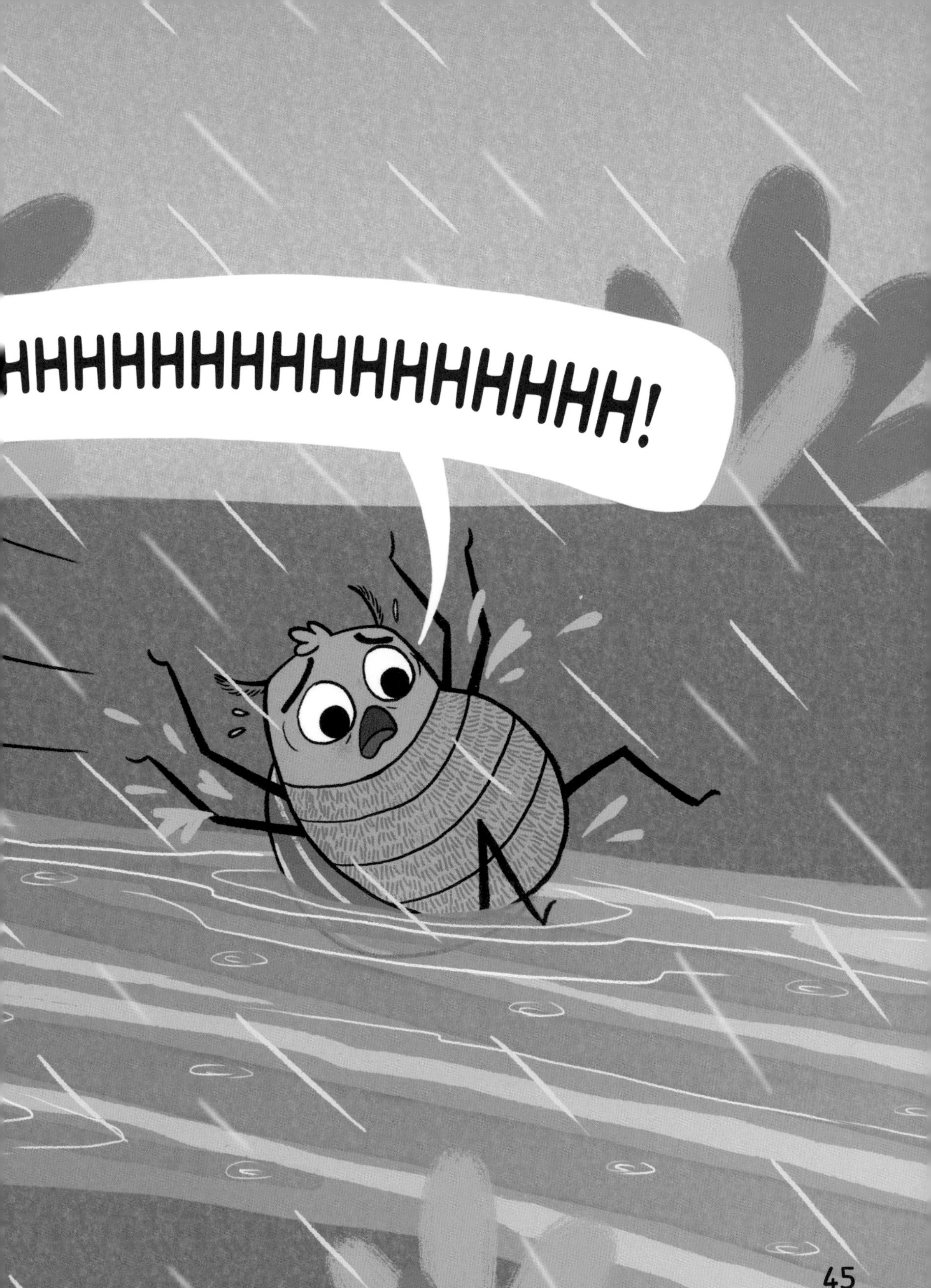
HHHHHHHHHHHHHHHH!

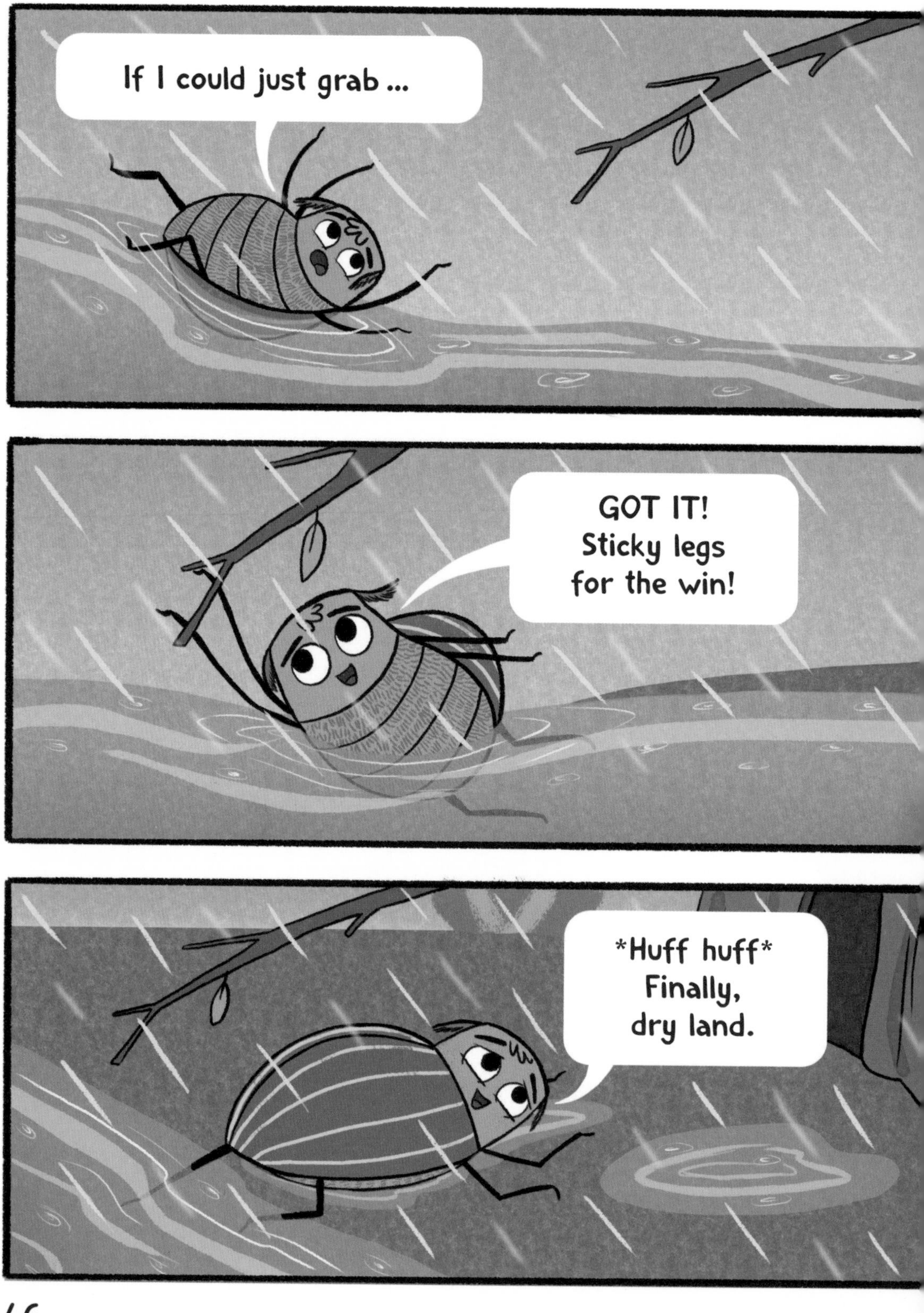
If I could just grab ...
GOT IT! Sticky legs for the win!
Huff huff Finally, dry land.

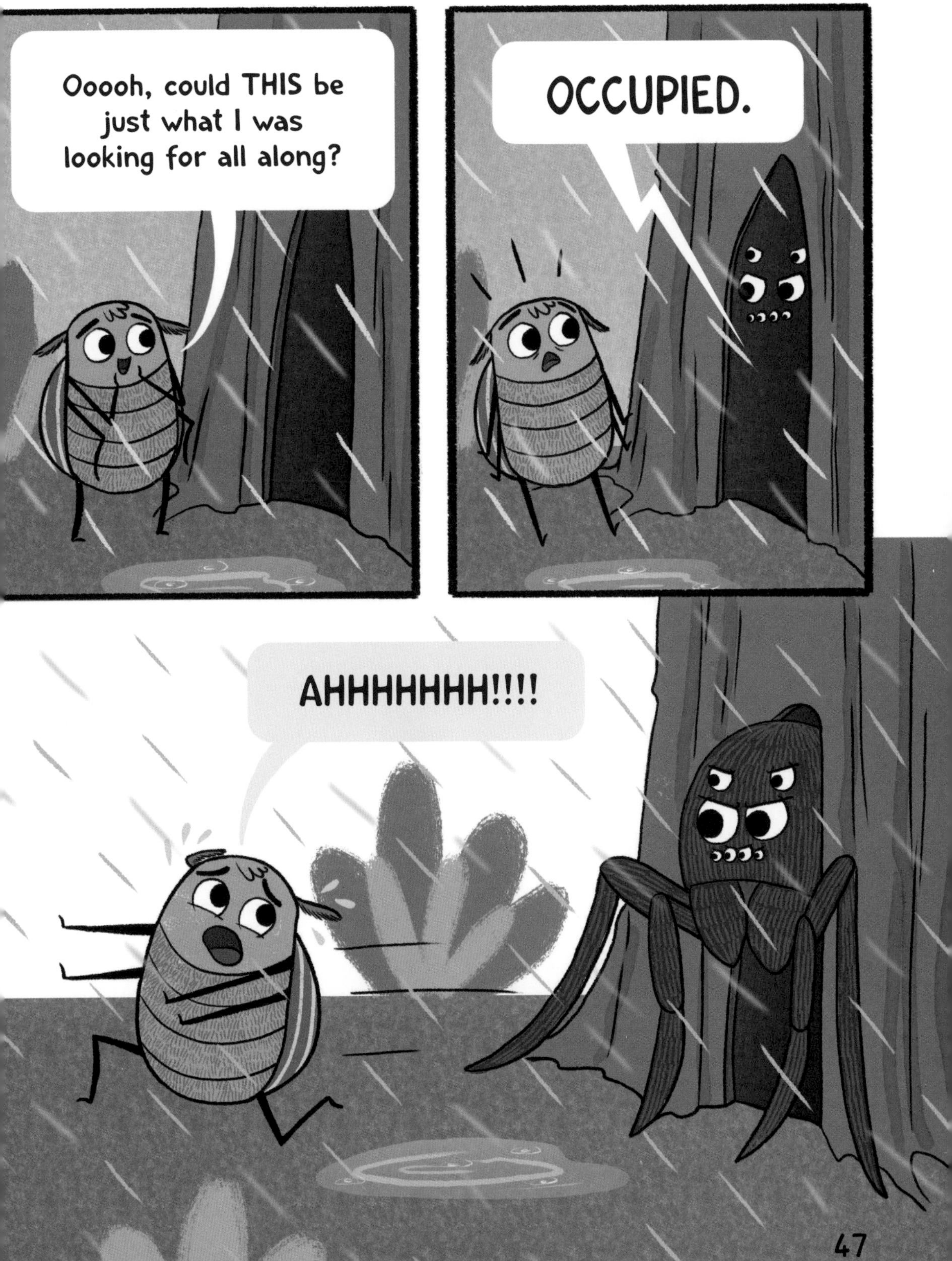
Ooooh, could THIS be just what I was looking for all along?
OCCUPIED.
AHHHHHHH!!!!

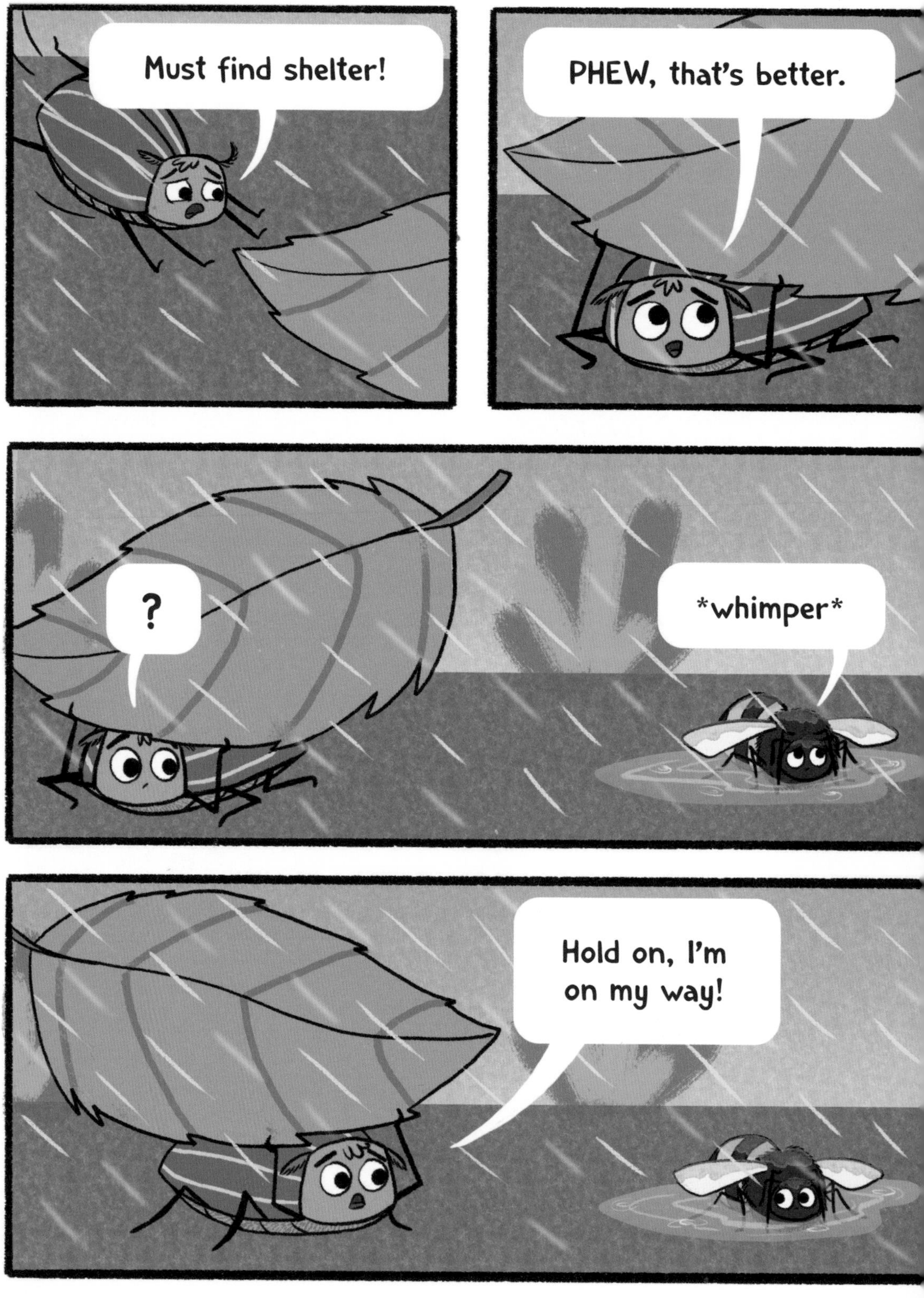

Must find shelter!
PHEW, that's better.
?
whimper
Hold on, I'm
on my way!

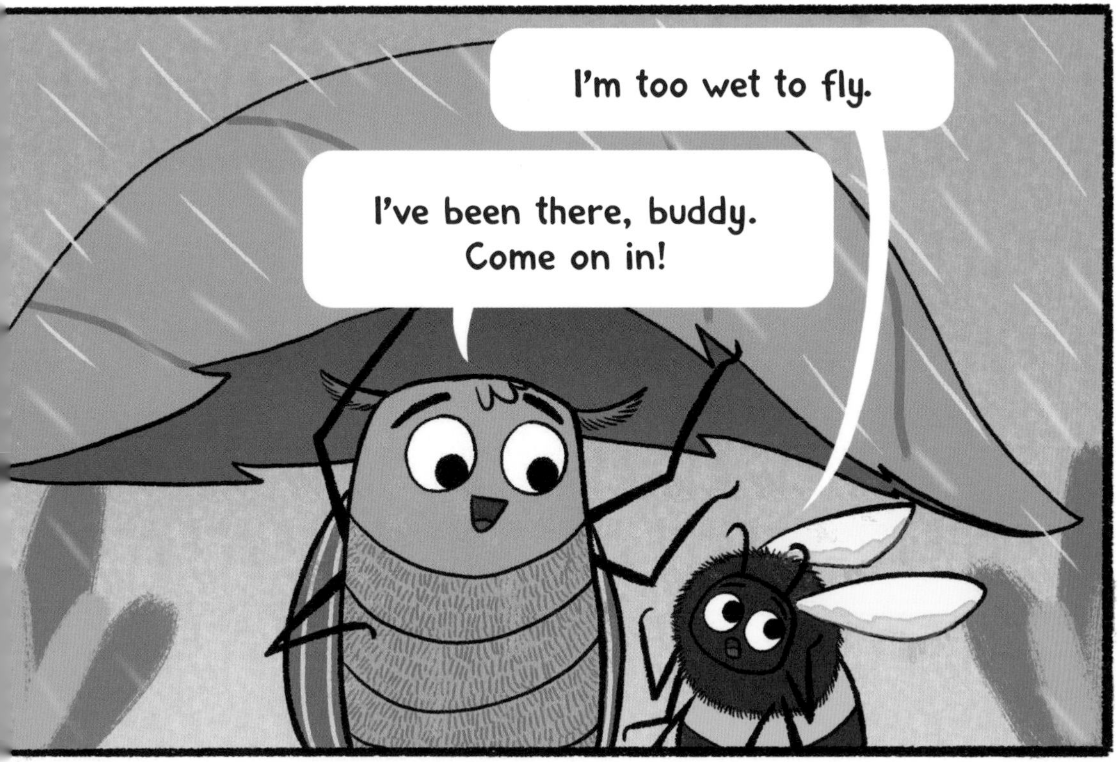
I'm too wet to fly.
I've been there, buddy. Come on in!

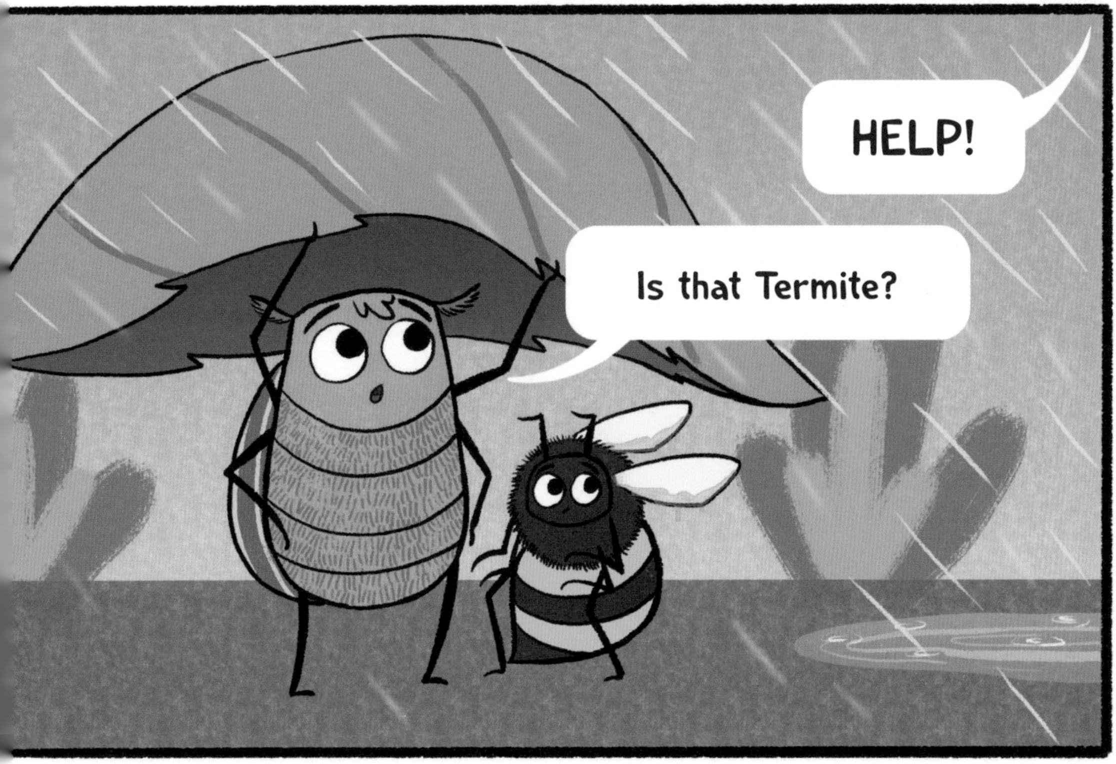
HELP!
Is that Termite?

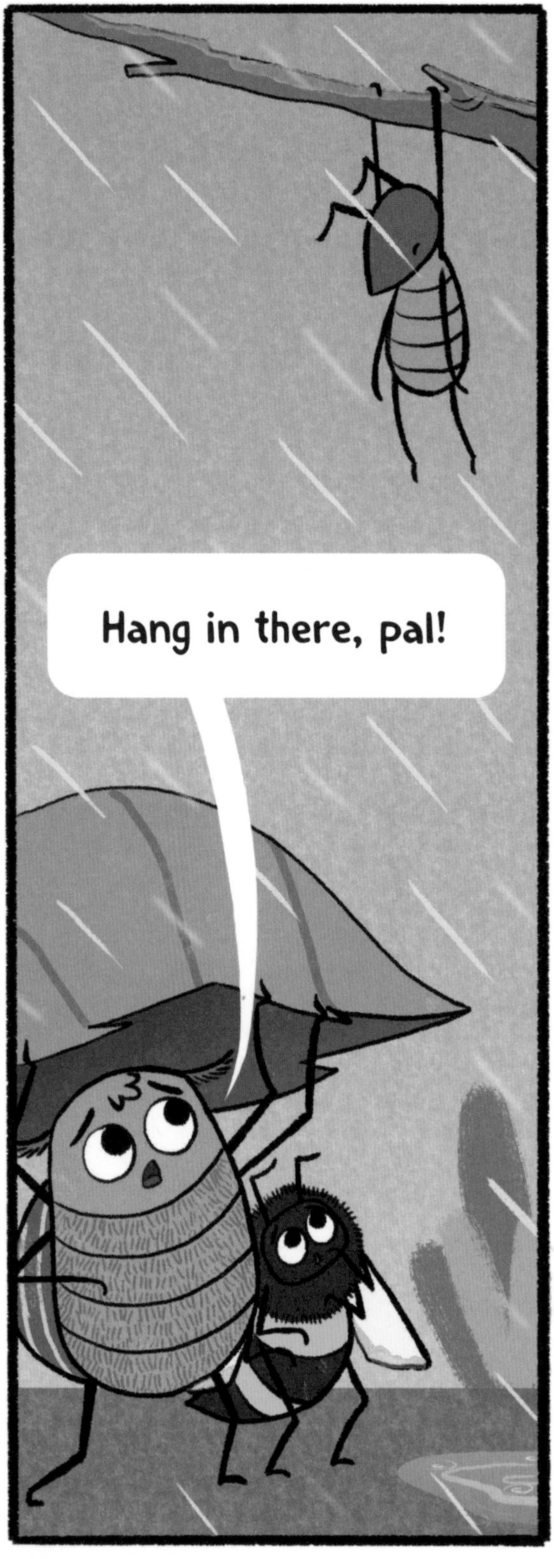
Hang in there, pal!

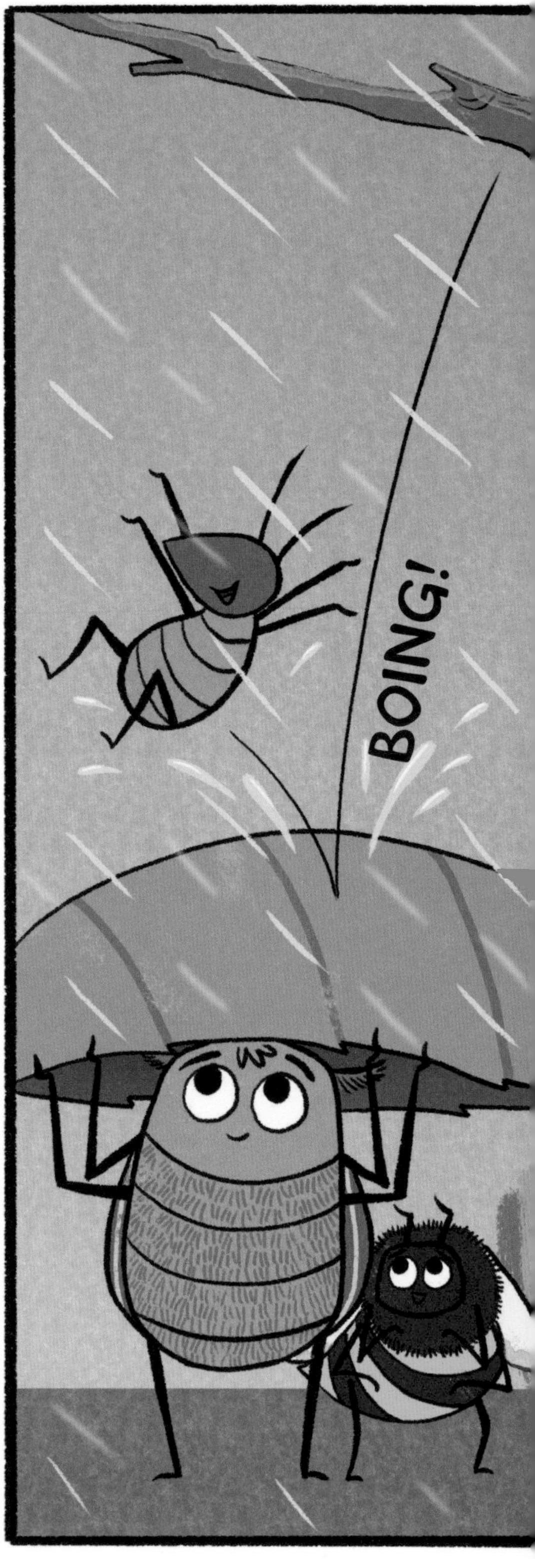
BOING!

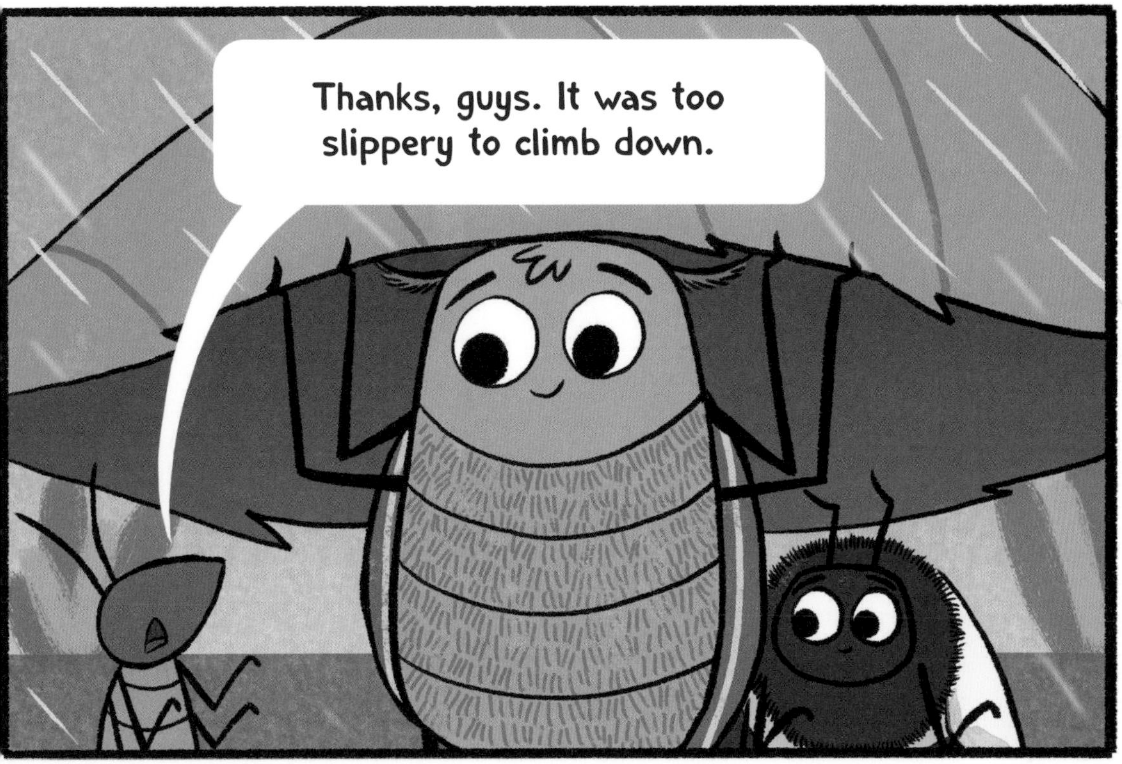
Thanks, guys. It was too slippery to climb down.

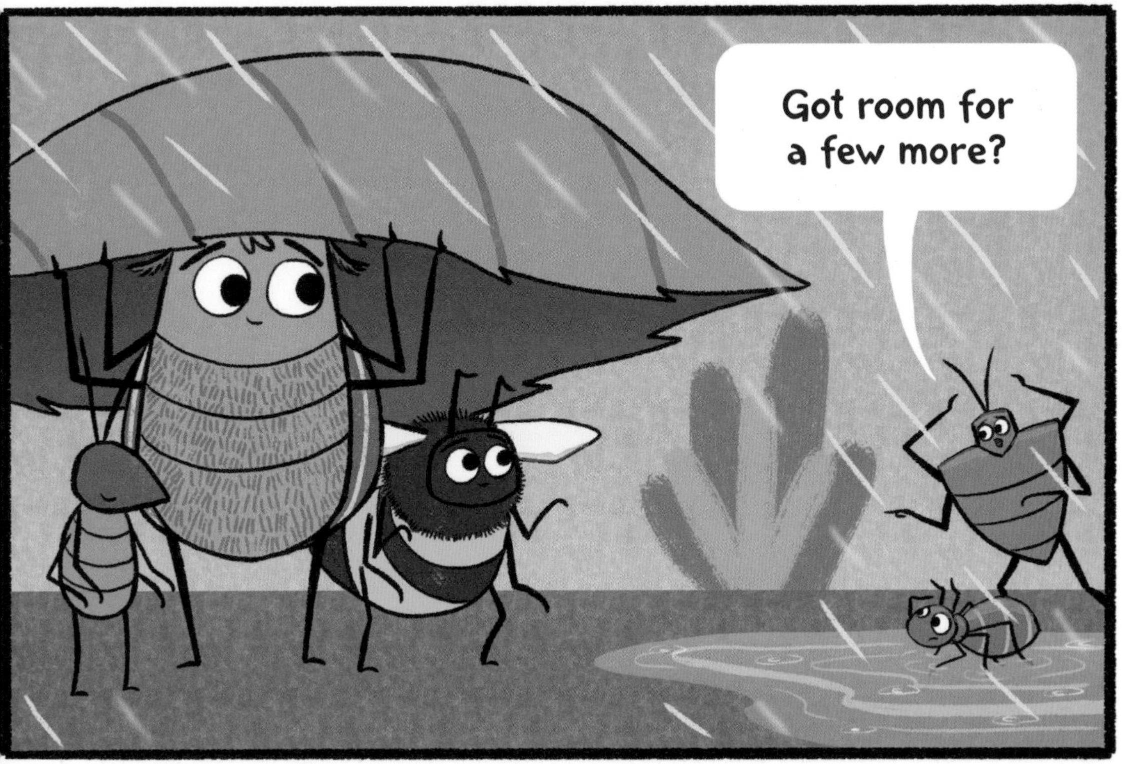
Got room for a few more?

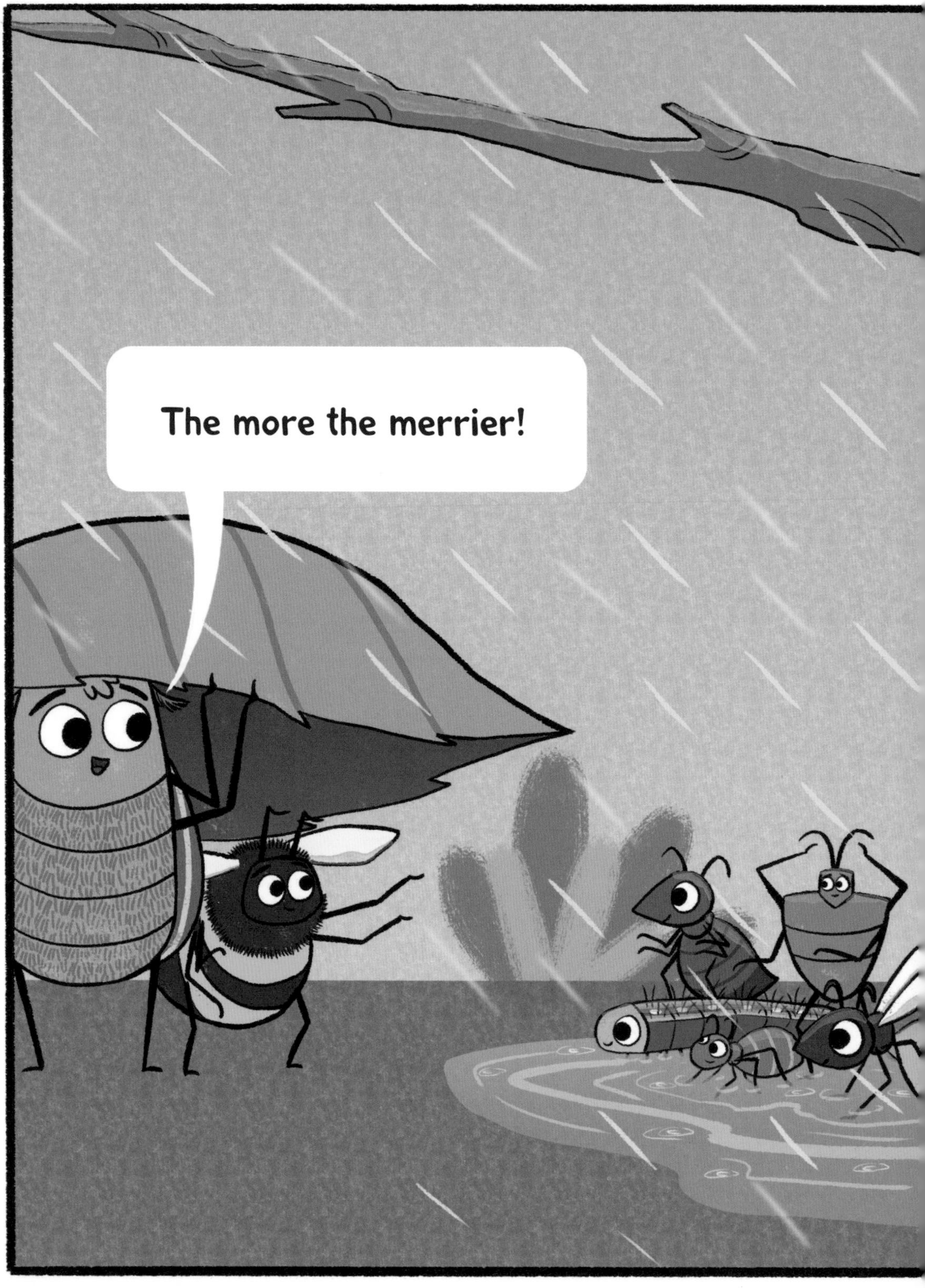
The more the merrier!

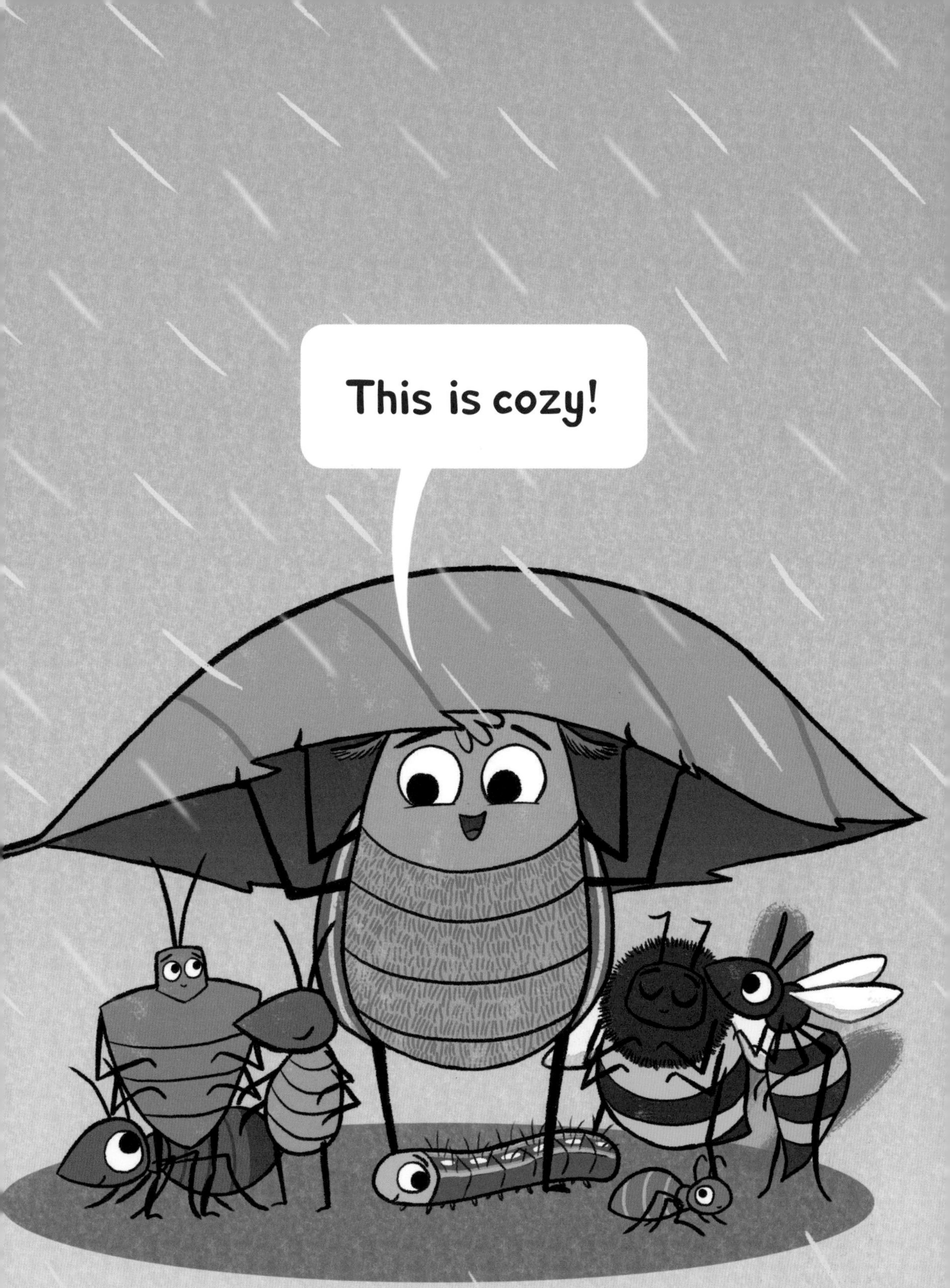
This is cozy!

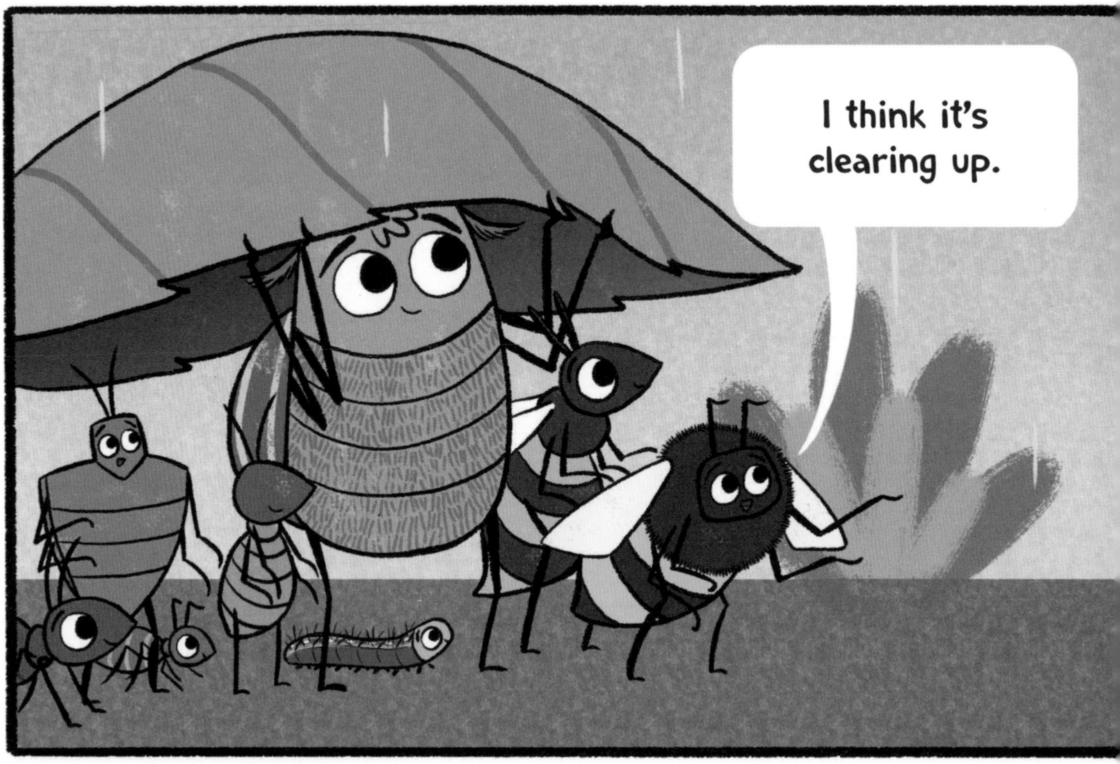
I think it's clearing up.

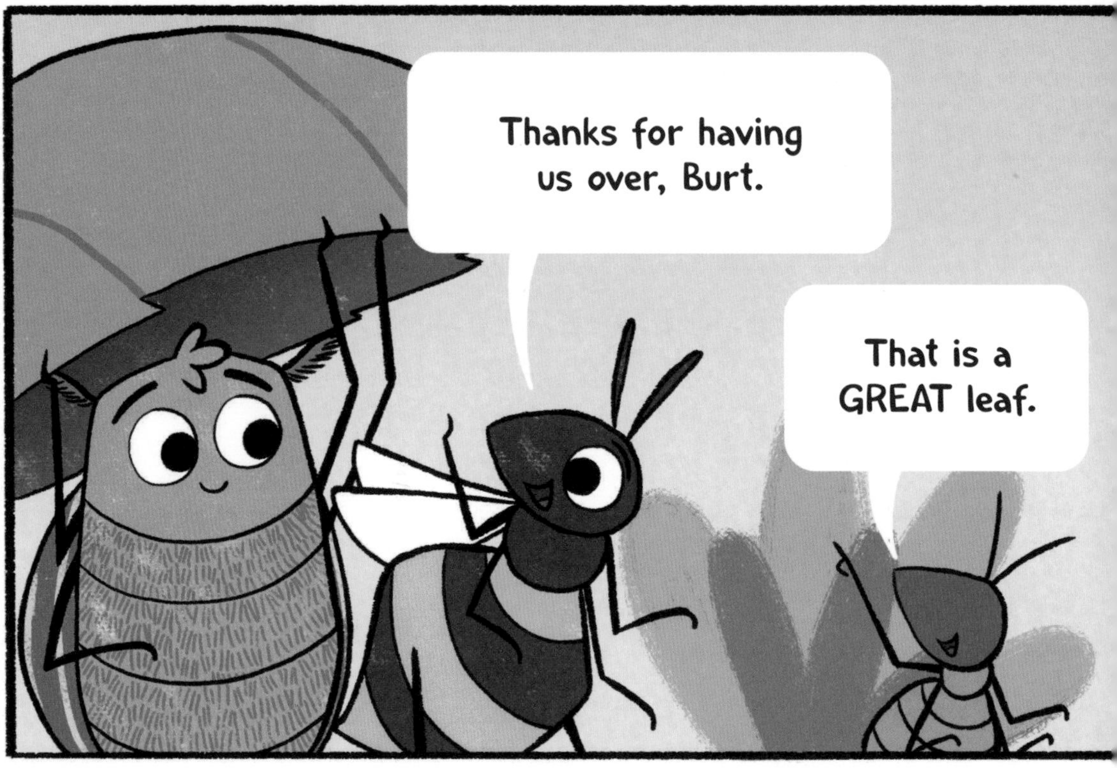
Thanks for having us over, Burt.
That is a GREAT leaf.

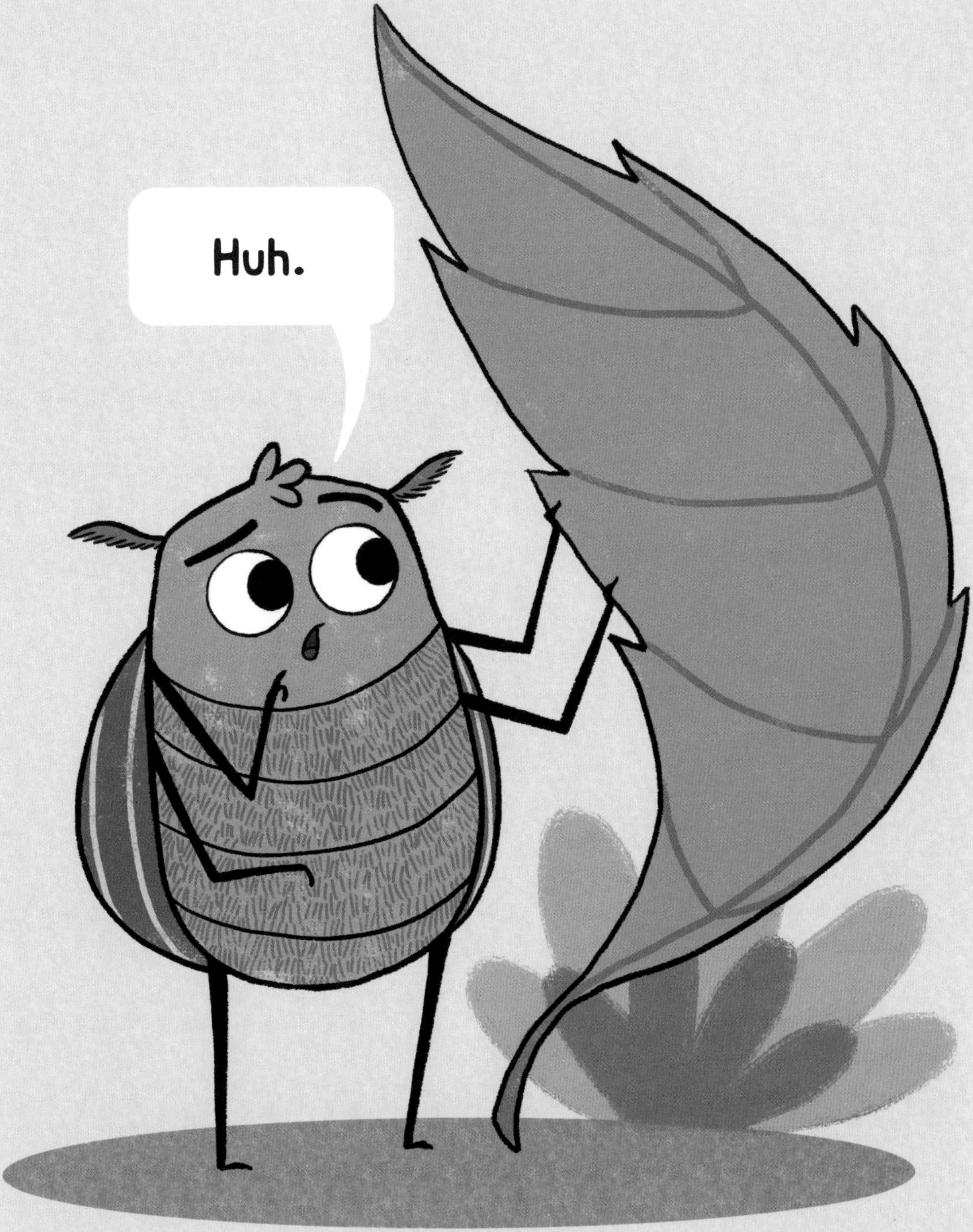
Huh.

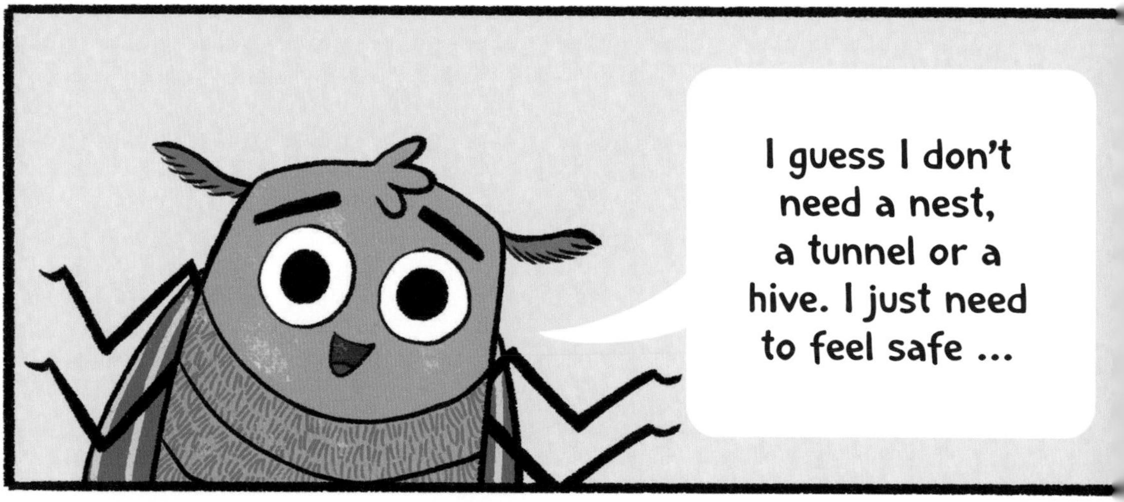
I guess I don't need a nest, a tunnel or a hive. I just need to feel safe ...

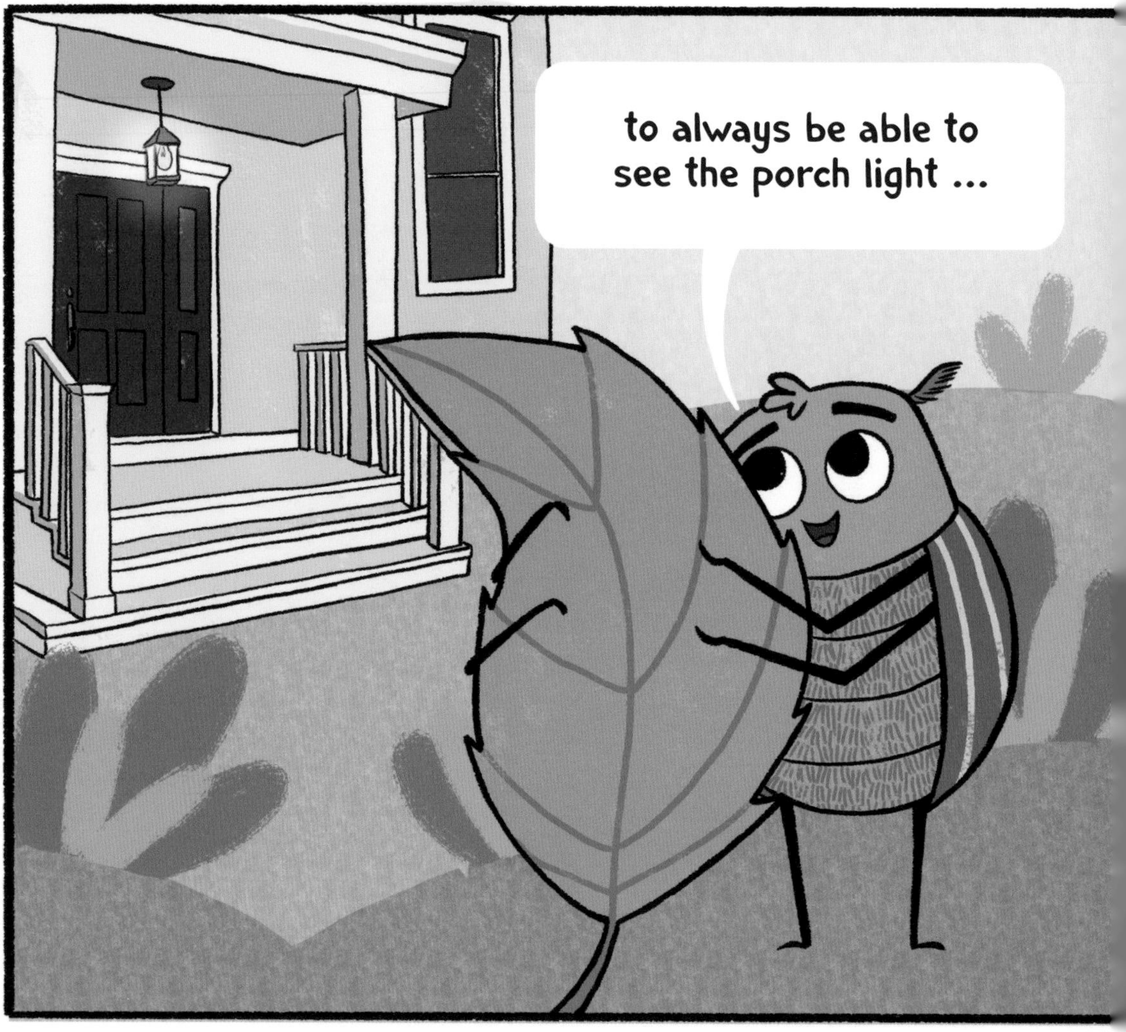
to always be able to see the porch light ...

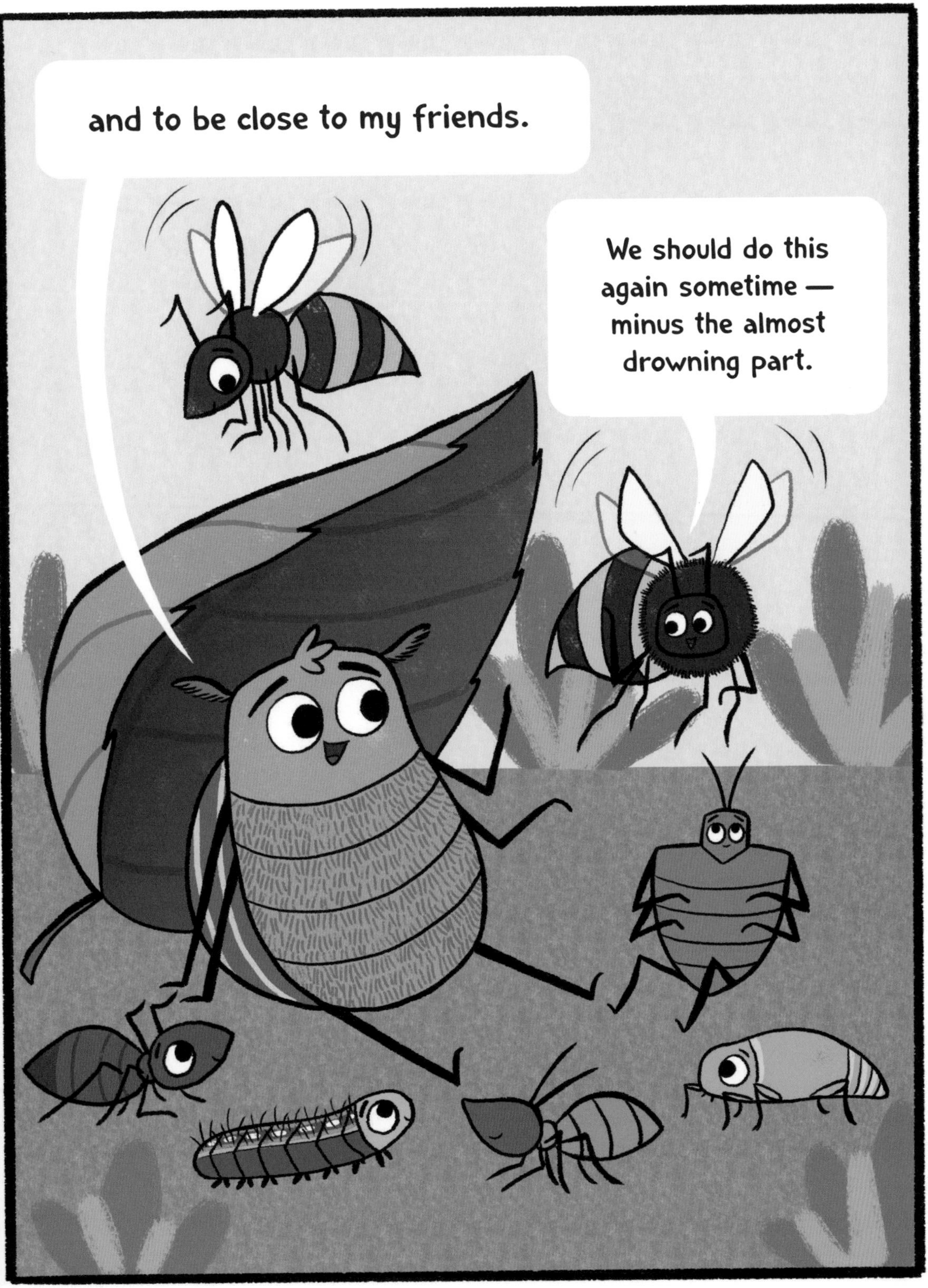
and to be close to my friends.
We should do this again sometime — minus the almost drowning part.

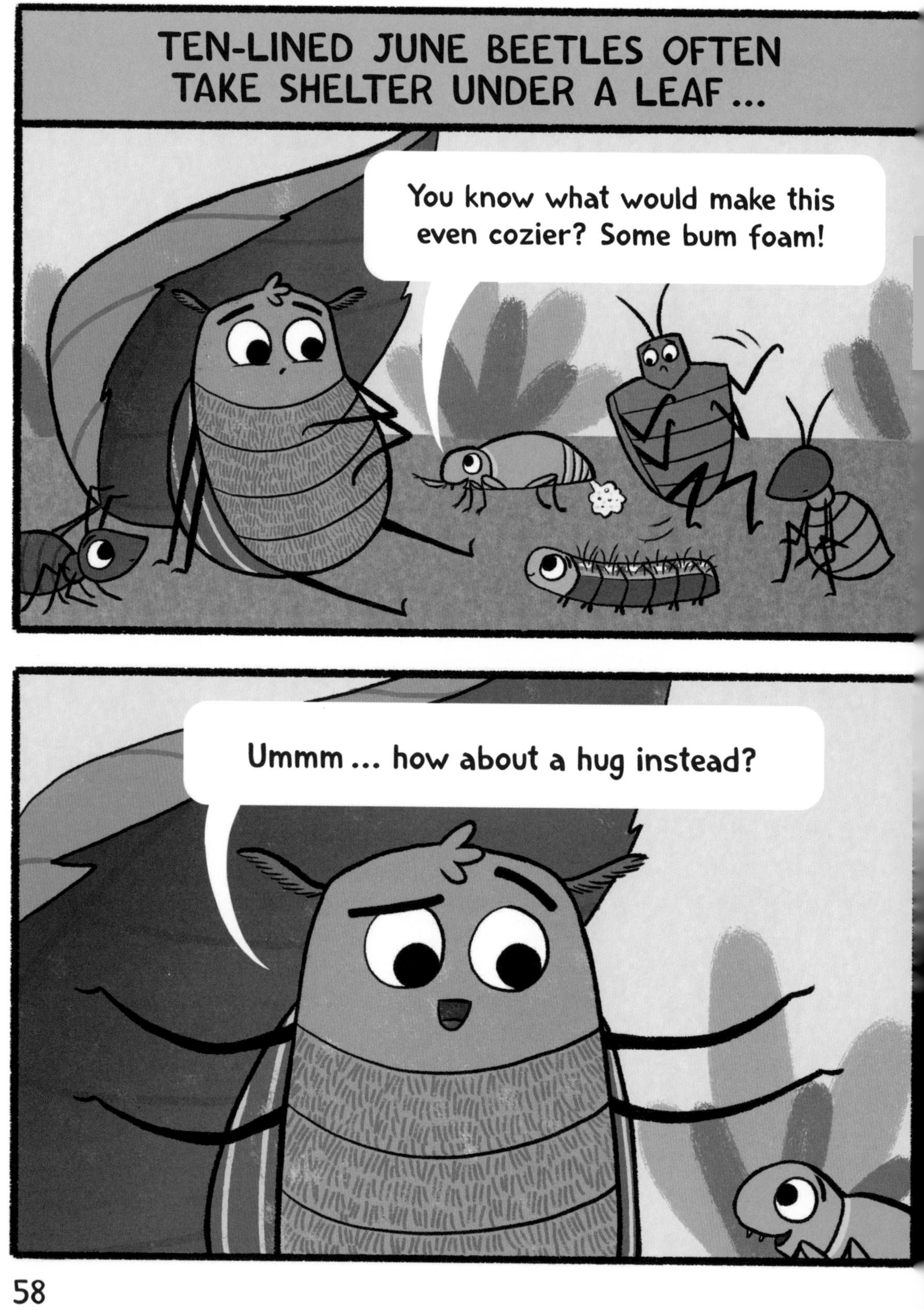
TEN-LINED JUNE BEETLES OFTEN TAKE SHELTER UNDER A LEAF...
You know what would make this even cozier? Some bum foam!
Ummm... how about a hug instead?

AND THEY WILL ALWAYS MAKE ROOM FOR THEIR FRIENDS.

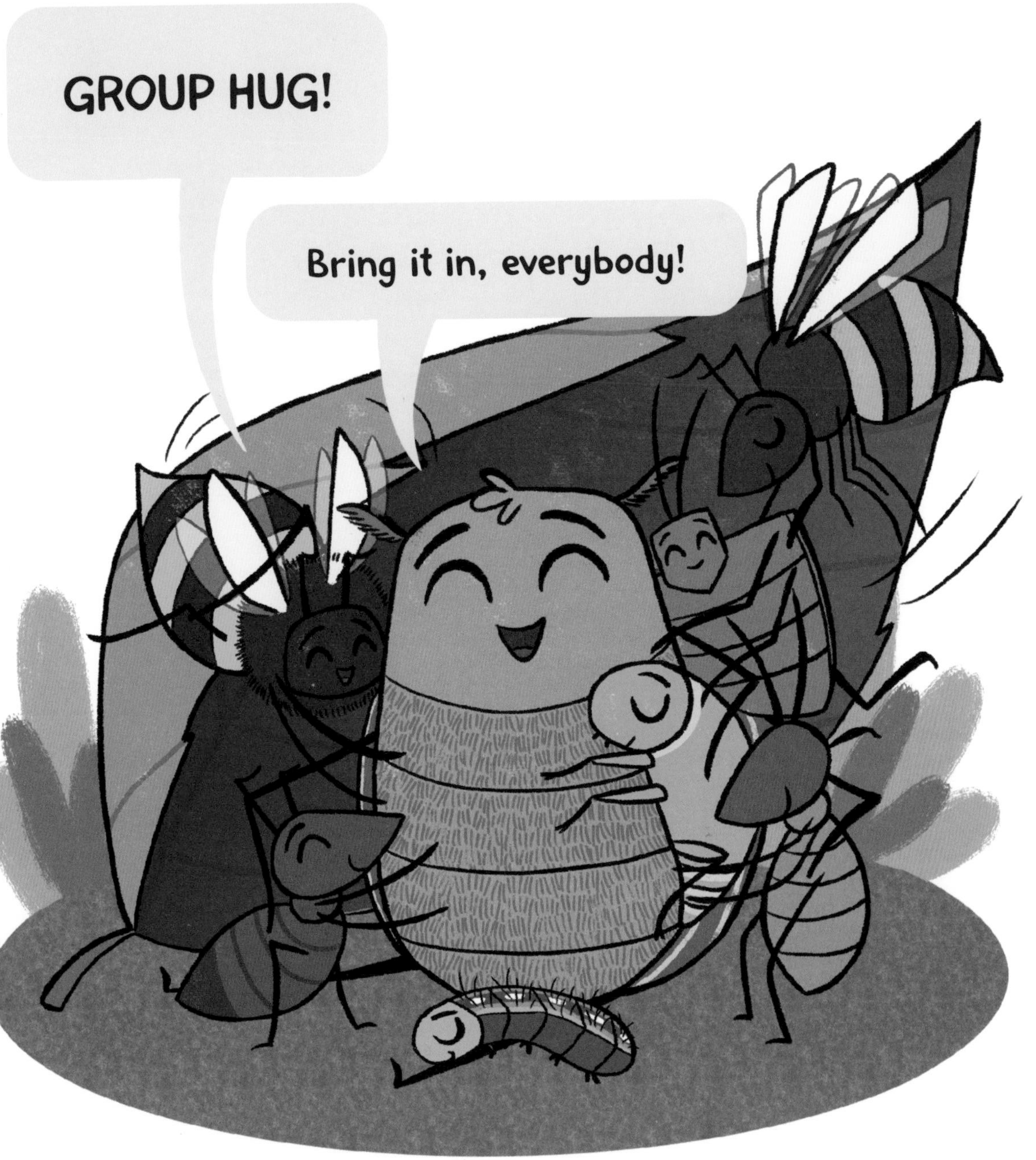
GROUP HUG!
Bring it in, everybody!

AWESOME INSECT **BUILDER** FACTS!

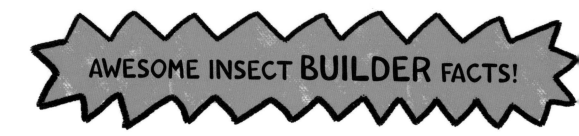

Leaf cutter ants live in underground nests that can grow to 60 meters (197 feet) across and house 8 million individuals, making them the largest animal society next to humans. They even maintain fungus gardens to feed their babies.

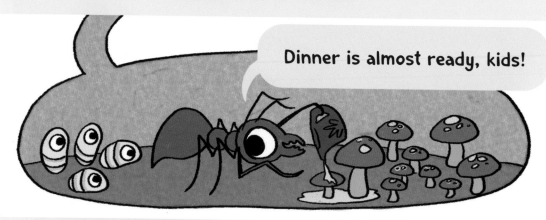

Dinner is almost ready, kids!

The caddisfly larva builds a portable protective case out of pieces of plants, sand grains, twigs and other items. They carry their home on their bodies while they grow.

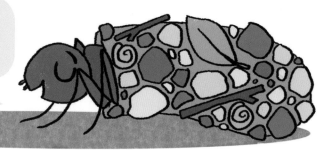

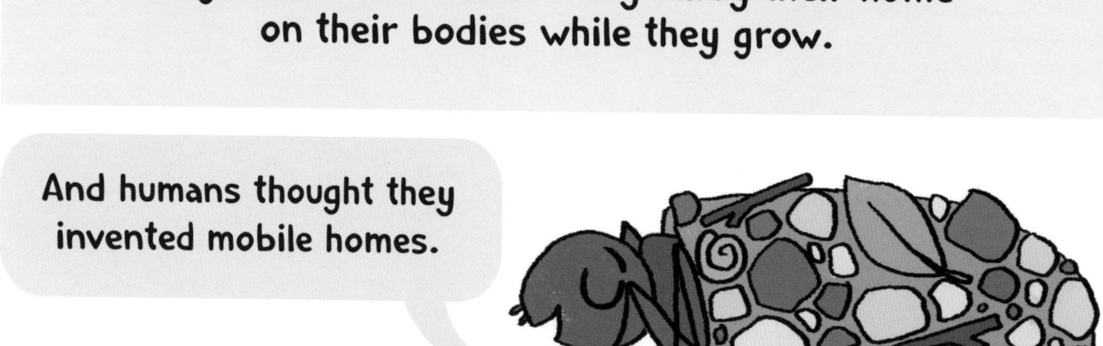

And humans thought they invented mobile homes.

Carpenter ants don't just build one home, they create whole neighborhoods! If their main home is attacked by a predator, they just move next door where it's safe.

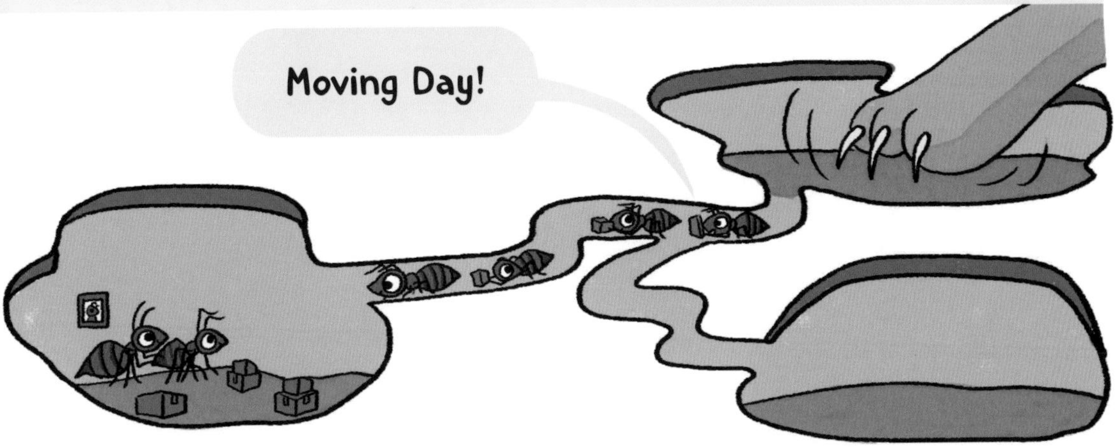
Moving Day!

While all of the 30 000 wasp species in the world use wood fibers to build their nests, the shape of their vespiaries (fancy word for wasp nests) varies depending on the species.

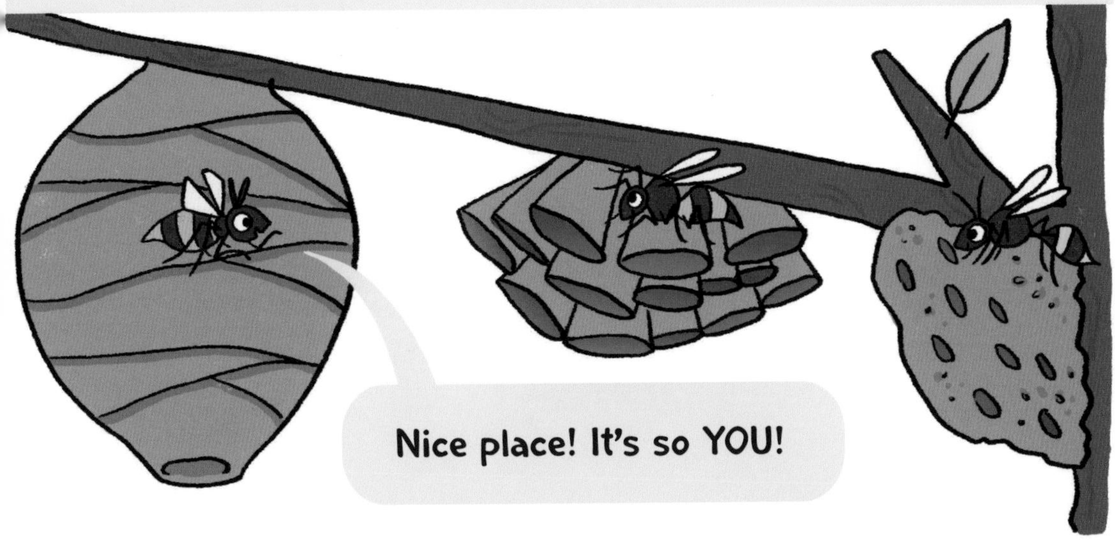
Nice place! It's so YOU!

Cathedral termites make towering mounds up to 8 meters (26 feet) high out of mud, plants, saliva and dung (poop). Their nest lies beneath the tall structure and can last 50–100 years.

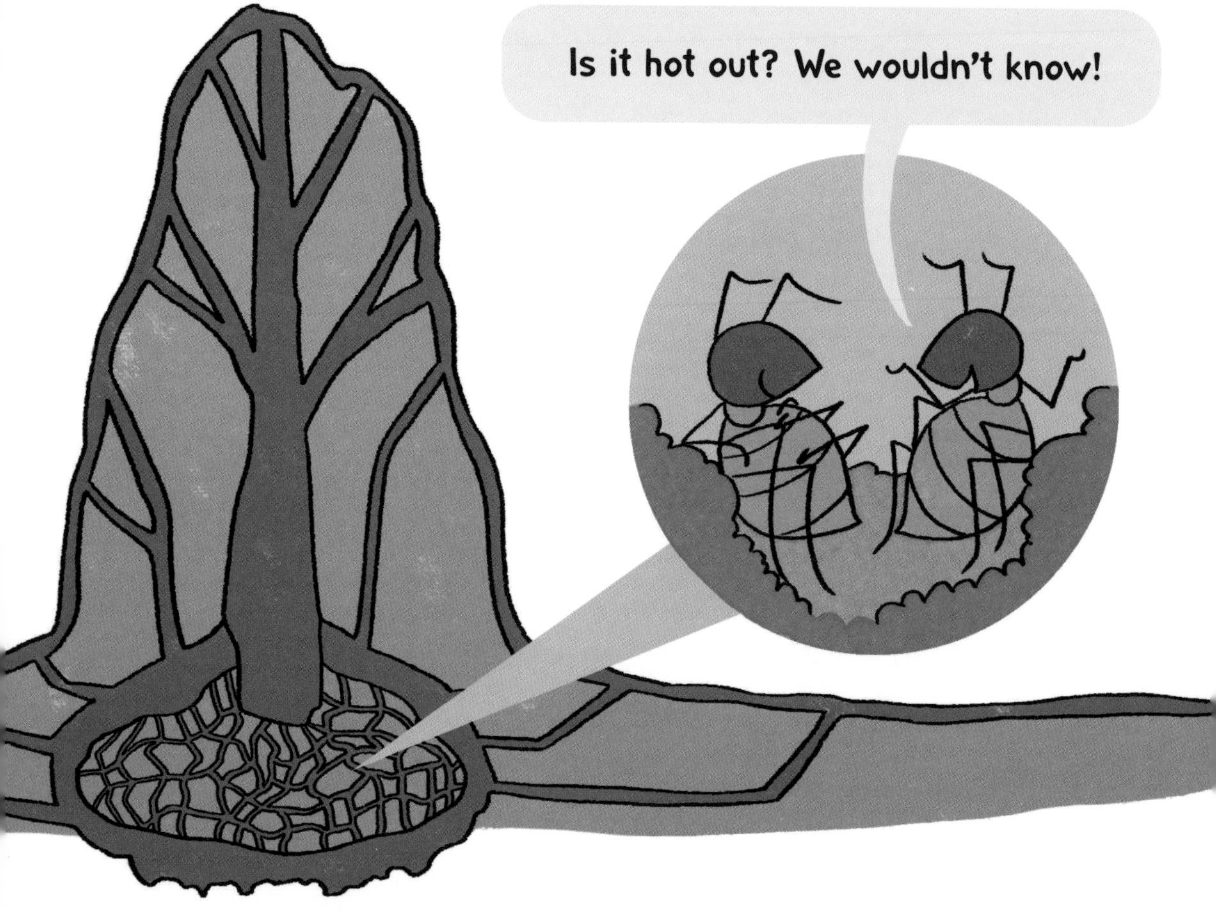
Is it hot out? We wouldn't know!

Their mounds have a central chimney connected to a network of small tunnels. Fresh air travels through the chimney, cooling the warm air within and providing the termites with their own air conditioning system.

Ants aren't just amazing at constructing nests. Army ants can build bridges out of their own bodies to help each other travel over gaps in the road.

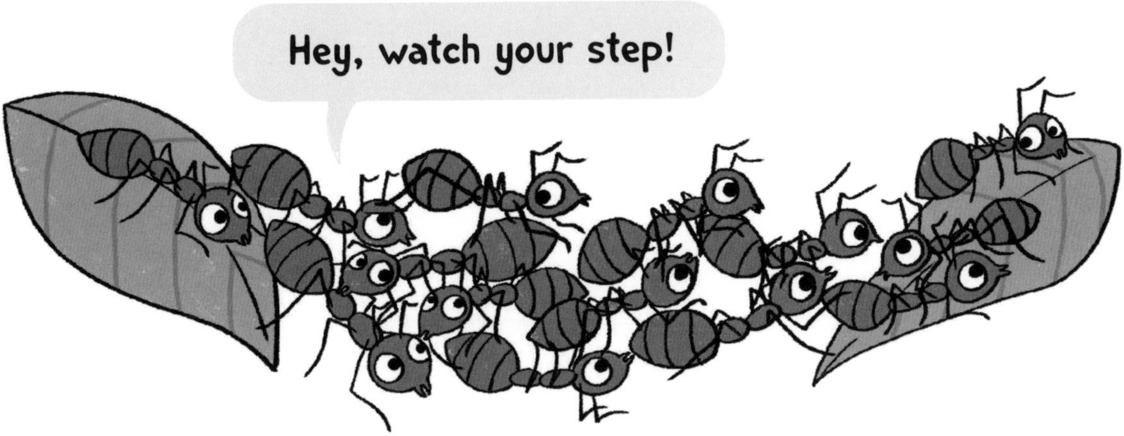
Hey, watch your step!

Honeybees build hexagons so perfect that mathematicians have been studying them for thousands of years. Humans only recently proved what bees have always known — the hexagon is the best shape to maximize space while using the least amount of wax.

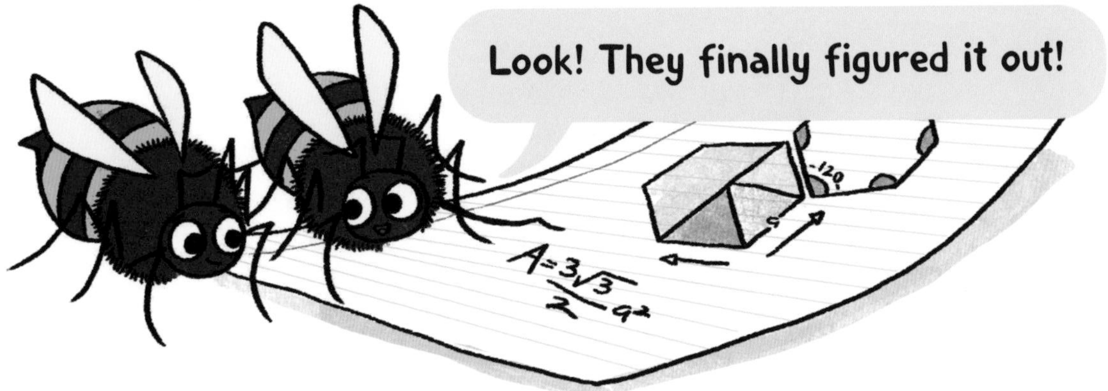
Look! They finally figured it out!

For all the wonderful people who
make my neighborhood my home

Text and illustrations ©2023 Ashley Spires

All rights reserved. No part of this publication may be reproduced, stored in aretrieval system or transmitted, in any form or by any means, without the prior written permission of Kids Can Press Ltd. or, in case of photocopying or other reprographic copying, a license from The Canadian Copyright Licensing Agency (Access Copyright). For an Access Copyright license, visit www.accesscopyright.ca or call toll free to 1-800-893-5777.

Published in Canada and the U.S. by Kids Can Press Ltd.
25 Dockside Drive, Toronto, ON M5A 0B5

Kids Can Press is a Corus Entertainment Inc. company

www.kidscanpress.com

The art in this book was rendered digitally under
the shelter of a particularly great air-conditioned leaf.
The text is set in Comical.

Edited by Yasemin Uçar
Designed by Karen Powers

Printed and bound in Shenzhen,
China, in 10/2022 by C & C Offset

CM 23 0 9 8 7 6 5 4 3 2 1

FSC
www.fsc.org
MIX
Paper | Supporting
responsible forestry
FSC® C008047

Library and Archives Canada Cataloguing in Publication

Title: Burt the Beetle lives here / Ashley Spires.
Names: Spires, Ashley, 1978– author, artist.
Identifiers: Canadiana 2022023261X | ISBN 9781525310119 (hardcover)
Subjects: LCGFT: Graphic novels.
Classification: LCC PN6733.S66 B89 2023 | DDC j741.5/971 — dc23

Kids Can Press gratefully acknowledges that the land on which our office is located is the traditional territory of many nations, including the Mississaugas of the Credit, the Anishnabeg, the Chippewa, the Haudenosaunee and the Wendat peoples, and is now home to many diverse First Nations, Inuit and Métis peoples.

We thank the Government of Ontario, through Ontario Creates; the Ontario Arts Council; the Canada Council for the Arts; and the Government of Canada for supporting our publishing activity.

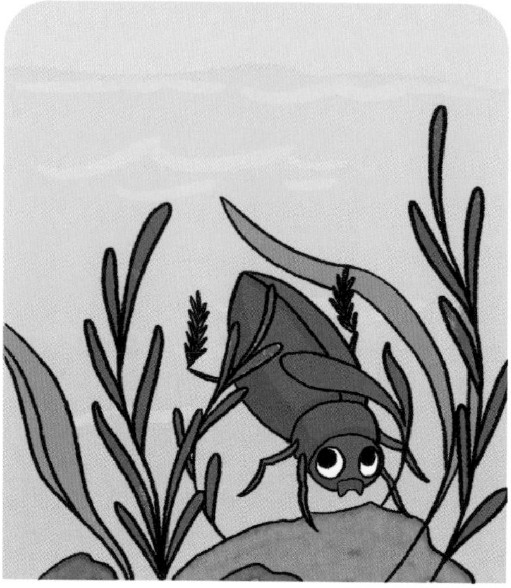

VIEWS OF THE WATER

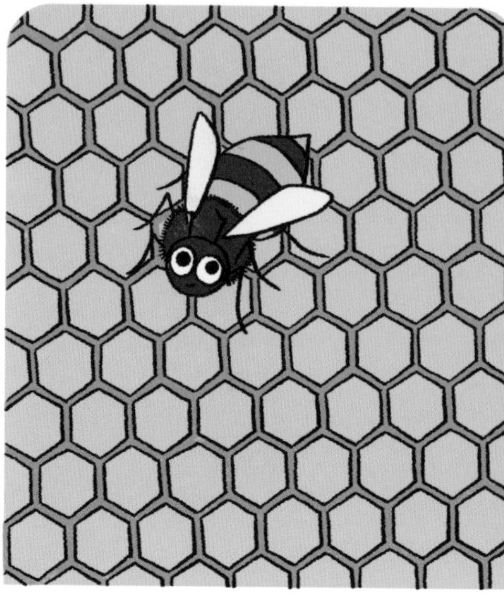

QUALITY CRAFTSMANSHIP

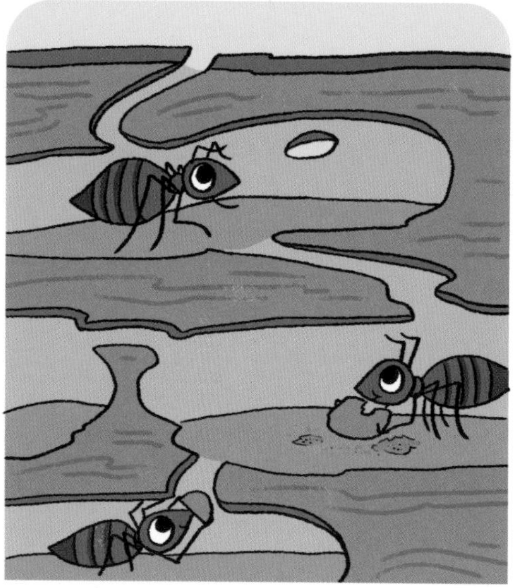

IMPECCABLY RENOVATED

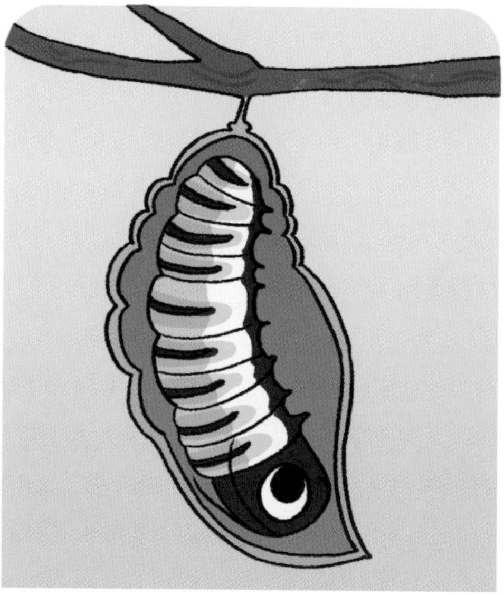

EASILY CONVERTED